YOU KNOW I'M NO GOOD

ALSO BY JESSIE ANN FOLEY

The Carnival at Bray
Neighborhood Girls
Sorry for Your Loss

YOU KNOW I'M NO GOOD

JESSIE ANN FOLEY

Quill Tree Books
An Imprint of HarperCollins Publishers

Quill Tree Books is an imprint of HarperCollins Publishers.

You Know I'm No Good

Library of Congress Control Number: 2020937806
ISBN 978-0-06-295708-5

Typography by Catherine San Juan
20 21 22 23 24   PC/LSCH   10 9 8 7 6 5 4 3 2 1

First Edition

For Beth,
in loving memory

YOU KNOW I'M NO GOOD

ARRIVING

I TOLD YOU I WAS TROUBLE
YOU KNOW THAT I'M NO GOOD.

—AMY WINEHOUSE, "YOU KNOW I'M NO GOOD"

MY NAME IS MIA DEMPSEY, and I am a troubled teen.

I'm a sleep-with-random-boys-I-meet-in-the-Fullerton-underpass kind of troubled.

A 1.7-grade-point-average kind of troubled.

A stick-and-poke-heart-on-my-upper-left-boob kind of troubled.

A peppermint-schnapps-in-my-water-bottle-during-first-period-American-history kind of troubled.

A punch-my-stepmom kind of troubled.[1]

Of all the ways that I am troubled, it's this last one, so far as I can tell, that has landed me in here.

Maybe if I had just apologized to Alanna, I'd still be in my own room at home, surrounded by my books and journals, my laptop and my closetful of shoplifted clothes, instead of lying on this creaky aluminum bunk bed, staring up at rusty

---

[1] For the record, I didn't *punch* her, exactly. I hit her with my closed fist slightly harder than I meant to. I'd intended to, I don't know, *cuff* her on the shoulder, but she happens to be pretty short—five foot one to my five foot six—so I missed her shoulder and got her in the face instead. Yes, it probably hurt, and yes, her nose bled, kind of a lot, but it's not like bones were broken or anything.

springs while, above me, some weird stranger whimpers in her sleep.

But I am not good at apologizing.

For me, every time I try to say *I'm sorry* or *I love you*, the words dissolve on my tongue like tabs of emotional acid.

Still, in my defense, how could I apologize after what she said to me?

That day, as Alanna held the bag of frozen corn over her face, her lap piled high with bloody Kleenex, my dad—called home from work in the middle of the day once again to deal with a Mia Crisis—kept asking: *Why, Mia? Why? Why would you do this?*

I knew why, and so did Alanna, but I couldn't tell him. I couldn't repeat the words that had come out of her mouth and had triggered my fist, because I knew there was a chance he might agree with those words. And if he did, it would slice into me so deep I wasn't sure I'd be able to keep acting like I didn't care.

2

"TROUBLED TEEN." What a stupid phrase. First of all, you'll never catch any self-respecting human between the ages of thirteen and nineteen referring to herself as a "teen." "Kid," "girl," "person": those are all fine. "Teen," however, is a social construct, a word that should never be used to describe actual people but instead reserved for all those not-too-childish but also not-too-sophisticated products that adults in marketing meetings are always trying to convince us we can't live without: Fuzzy, utterly functionless beanbag chairs. Glittery phone cases. Rainbow-striped scrunchies. Crop tops that claim to be a size six but are actually the size of a Post-it note. Pretty much anything with pom-poms on it.

And "troubled"? To me, this is a word that brings to mind someone sitting in a library, staring off into space, thoughtfully stroking her chin as she ponders a difficult—a *troubling*—algebraic equation. I *wish* I were troubled. Instead, what I am is enraged.

At what, exactly, I couldn't tell you. The world, my place in it, and everyone who populates it—does that narrow it down? Anyway, it doesn't matter, since "Red Oak Academy: A Therapeutic Girls' Boarding School for Chronically Pissed-Off Humans Between the Ages of Thirteen and Nineteen" doesn't flow off the tongue nearly as well as "Red Oak Academy: A Therapeutic Girls' Boarding School for *Troubled Teens*."

Seriously, what is it with adults and their euphemisms? Why are they so terrified of calling things what they actually are? For example, why does Alanna get all bent out of shape when I call Lauren and Lola my half sisters? *Why can't you drop the "half"?* she asks. *They're just your sisters.* But that isn't true. It's not like I don't love the twins, but the fact is, they came out of Alanna's vagina, and I didn't. End of story.

And why have all my teachers insisted, since I was six years old, in calling me "gifted"? I'm not gifted. I'm just smart. I read a ton, I test well, and I like writing almost as much as I like cutting class to smoke weed in the parking lot behind the bankrupt Sears at Six Corners. So what? What does "gifted" even mean? How is it a gift, being bored as fuck at school my whole life, having to pretend to fumble over words like "prodigious" and "irrelevant" when I'm asked to read aloud so the other kids won't think I'm a freak? Feeling like my brain is always cranking, like it can never shut off, like the only thing that can calm it down is to inhale a book or a drug or a boy?

"Perhaps Mia is troubled *because* she's so gifted."

This was Mr. Cullerton's brilliant assessment of me when I had my last suspension hearing.

"Or maybe," Alanna had said, because she just couldn't help herself, "it's because of what happened to her mother."

And that's the thing. Alanna gets all butthurt that I won't drop the "half" from "half sisters" when I talk about Lauren and Lola. But she has never once asked me to call her Mom.[2] She loves bringing up the stuff with my real mom, because for her, it ties everything up in a nice little package. It gives an explanation for why I am the way I am, because if there's one thing adults love, even more than euphemisms, it's the concept of cause and effect. If Alanna and my dad can believe that what happened to my mother is the cause, and my being a Troubled Teen™ is the effect, then they can avoid the two alternative explanations: (1) that people like me are just born bad for no reason at all; or (2) that *they* made me the way I am, by some central mistake in how they raised me. You don't have to be gifted to see why it's easier to simply blame it all on a dead woman and move on.

---

[2] Not that I ever would, of course, even if she *did* ask.

3

YOU DON'T WIND UP at a therapeutic boarding school until you have run entirely out of second chances and your parents have run entirely out of patience.[3] I'll be the first to admit that Dad and Alanna tried plenty of other tactics before it came to this: phone restrictions and confiscations, curfews, grounding, consequence charts, behavioral contracts, chore wheels, sending me to volunteer at a soup kitchen, sending me to pound nails and carry wood at my uncle's contracting job. This is not to mention all the consequences I got at school—attendance contracts, detentions, in-school and out-of-school suspensions, endless lectures from teachers about "wasted potential;" not to mention all the various therapists I've been sent to since *what happened to my mother* happened; not to *mention* all the drugs said therapists have put me on over the years—Adderall and Ritalin and Zoloft and Ativan—and those are just the ones I

---

[3] But they better not be out of money. Guess how much this place costs? Six thousand dollars. A *month*. If Dad and Alanna want to blow their retirement savings and the twins' college funds to send me on a trip to teen prison, I guess that's their own dumb business.

can name off the top of my head.

But none of it worked.

I'm still me.

I'm still bad.

So now I'm here.

4

WHEN YOU ARE SENT to a therapeutic boarding school like this one, there is no orientation, the way you might have at a normal high school. That's because there is no regular start date to the school year. Every girl arrives at a different time, at whatever point in the year her troubledness becomes too troubling for those around her to deal with anymore.

So they don't call it orientation. They call it intake, which sounds much more clinical and scary because, as I soon learned, it *is* much more clinical and scary.

My intake occurred in the middle of October my junior year, three days after I punched Alanna in the face.

It was a Saturday, and I'd spent it as I often had over the past few months, hanging out with Xander.

Xander is my Xanax dealer.

Yes, you heard that right.

Xander is also—well, I guess *was* also, since I now live several hundred miles away from him and don't have access to Wi-Fi—someone I hooked up with from time to time. One of those times happened to be the same day Alanna forgot her lunch in the fridge. She stopped home from the school where she teaches to grab it, which is how she stumbled upon Xander and me under a blanket on the family room couch when we should have been in fifth-period Spanish. Xander pulled up his pants and literally just ran for it, which left me naked and alone with a very angry stepmother who had now forgotten, for the second time that day, all about her Tupperware of minestrone soup. That's when she said the thing she said. And then I punched her. And then, three days later: intake.

5

XANDER IS THE RICHEST KID in school. His dad is from Germany and owns a semipro basketball team in Düsseldorf, which is why he has a full-sized basketball court in his basement with the team's logo—a snowy owl with its wings spread wide—painted onto the floor in the middle of center court. This is ironic because Xander himself failed PE last year, as did I, which is actually how we met. Coach Townsend was making our class run the mile, but neither Xander nor I would do it. For a week straight, we both refused to change into our gym uniforms. Coach was more confused than angry at our behavior.

Every day he'd say to us, "You guys know you have to run the mile to pass gym, right?"

We'd nod.

Then he'd say, "So, basically, by choosing not to complete this one simple task, you are ensuring your failure of this course."

We'd nod.

"And there's nothing I can do to help you from here on out."

We'd nod again, this time sympathetically, just so he understood it was nothing personal. We both liked Coach Townsend well enough; we just didn't feel like running the mile. Shaking his bald head, Coach would then jog off, and Xander and I would spend the next forty-five minutes sitting together in the bleachers, flirting happily while the other kids ran around the gym, showing off for each other like unneutered cocker spaniels at the Westminster dog show.

It goes without saying that Xander hates his dad. Kids like Xander *always* hate their dads. But actually, I'm a fan of Mr. Konig. Not that I've ever met him or anything; he works, like, ninety hours a week. I just like the idea of him—I like his style. I like the fact that the basketball court isn't even the most ostentatious aspect of his home, or even of his basement. That designation goes to the wine cellar, which is adjacent to the basketball court, just off the laundry room. It's a wide space, dimly lit, with limestone walls and carefully regulated cool air that smells like crushed grapes and money. There are so many rare bottles of wine in there that there's actually a code to open the door.[4] A guy like Mr. Konig could choose to donate his cash to cancer hospitals or famine relief or even snowy owls, which I'm pretty sure are endangered, but what does he do with it instead? He stockpiles expensive booze. He doesn't even try to pretend like he's a good person, which

---

[4] Which Xander figured out how to crack long ago. Say what you want about us troubled teens, but you can never say we're not resourceful. Especially when illicit substances are involved.

makes him different from most other adults I know. Give me an unapologetic greed monster over a hypocrite any day.

On this particular night, the night of my intake, Xander was furious because he'd just learned that his dad had kicked him off the family phone plan.

"He says I'm spoiled and I've never had to work for anything and I don't understand the value of money," Xander fumed. "Well, who does he think *made* me this way?"

"You know," I said, "things haven't been so great at my house, either, since my stepmom walked in on us. Thanks for asking, though."

"Sorry, sorry," he said, running two hands through his wild Teutonic curls. "*God.* I hate the way they control us." He drummed his fingers on the polished hardwood of the basketball court, then leaped up suddenly.

"Come on!" He grabbed me by the hand and pulled me to my feet. "I have an idea."

"What is it?"

"We're gonna drink my birthday bottle tonight."

"Wait—I thought your birthday was in March."

"It *is*. I'm talking about my birthday *bottle*."

I was confused.

"When I was a baby," he explained, leading me across the court toward the wine cellar, "my parents bought this French Bordeaux that was bottled the year I was born. It's been down here aging ever since. The idea is you open it on your twenty-first birthday and it's supposed to be this way of starting your adulthood with something beautiful and rare and classy instead of, I don't know, ten shots of Fireball or whatever."

"God," I said. "That's—I mean, that's kind of cool. Do you really want to ruin that over a phone plan?"

"Yes." He tapped the code into the security system and pulled open the door. "Screw him. And anyway, it's already been aged seventeen years. It's still going to possess a gorgeous mouthfeel."

I rolled my eyes. I had no idea what "mouthfeel" meant, but I certainly wasn't going to give Xander the satisfaction of asking. He loved to show off his wine knowledge to me because oenology was one of the very few fields that he knew more about than I did. He rummaged around the wall until he found the bottle, coated in a fine layer of dust. Rubbing it with the hem of his polo, he explained to me that back in the year of our birth, the Bordeaux region of France was incredibly hot—crazy, record-breaking hot—and also incredibly dry, with droughts that didn't break until mid-August. This meant that most of the wines from that year and that region turned out to be crap. But *this* one, he said, was meant to be, for complex reasons having to do with clay and soil and shade and shadow, utterly sublime.

"I don't think we should do this," I told him. "By the time you turn twenty-one, you might not hate your dad anymore."

But it was too late. Xander had already sliced off the foil at the top and was attacking the cork with an opener he'd lifted off a hook on the wall. There were crystal-stemmed glasses above us, hanging upside down and twinkling like chandeliers, but he took the first swig straight from the bottle.

"Whoa," he said, handing it to me and closing his eyes as he swallowed. "*Incroyable*."

If someone had told Xander that twenty-year-aged Cheetos were a delicacy, he would have eaten a handful and had the same reaction. The thing about Xander was that he had no mind of his own—no real taste. I thought to myself, as I took the bottle from him, that I couldn't wait to get out into the world, the big world, the world outside of high school, where I could meet guys who actually knew something about life and didn't have to fake it.

I took a long drink of the stuff, and you know what I tasted?

Dirt.

Heat.

Dry wind.

Gravel and clay and loam and worms.

I know, it sounds disgusting, right?

It wasn't.

It was, in fact, *incroyable*.

I kept thinking, as we passed the bottle back and forth, our lips and tongues staining red, that this Bordeaux from

France was bottled when Xander and I were just a couple of newborns who'd never hurt anyone or done anything wrong, who were made of nothing but love and milk and hope and promise. The wine was an inversion of us. It just kept getting better and better, while Xander and I kept getting worse and worse.

By the time the bottle was empty, the heat and dirt and clay of it had settled directly in my head, so that when we had sex on the floor of the wine cellar I moaned dutifully, even though I could barely feel it. Afterward, we split a joint, a king-sized bag of Twizzlers, and a couple benzos Xander had stolen from his mother. Then I walked home by myself, bare-armed in the October rain, too fucked-up to feel the cold, and passed out in the basement before the soothing pink flicker of Real Housewives reruns.

6

THE BIRTHDAY BOTTLE and the pills and the weed and maybe even the overdose of licorice all contributed to the fact that I wasn't able to fight back very well when the transport men came for me.

I'm not joking—that's their official title. Transport Men. Like we're living in a Marvel franchise or something.

I thought I was dreaming when they grabbed me at first, their voices soothing but their grips firm. By the time my brain had caught up to my circumstances, it was too late to do anything about it. I was already strapped into the back of what I now know was the Red Oak Academy Abductionmobile, and out the window I could see Dad and Alanna, Lauren and Lola, huddled together at the end of the driveway.

They were all crying.

My mouth was dry, and my head throbbed. I started to pound on the window—why was my family just standing there, letting me be kidnapped? Why weren't they calling 911? And then I became aware of a person twisted around from the front passenger seat, watching me. She had close-set, intelligent eyes; an incongruously delicate nose; and the kind of short utilitarian haircut, threaded throughout with wiry gray strands, that is so unapologetically ugly it feels like a political statement. The words she was speaking with narcotic calmness began to fall into order like metal shots in a pinball machine—*Red Oak Academy . . . I'm Dr. . . . but you can call me Mary Pat . . . help you need . . . a new chance . . . pain . . . therapeutic school . . . who you are and who you're meant to be.*

I couldn't process all of it, but I understood enough to know that the reason my family wasn't doing anything to thwart my kidnappers was because they were the ones who had called them. The betrayal of it all doubled me over. I'd punched Alanna first, but as it turned out, she punched back much harder. I'd heard about these kinds of places but had always believed them to be just another myth in the toolbox of lies parents use to control their kids, in the vein of *If you eat too much candy your teeth will fall out* or *Keep making that face and it will freeze like that forever.*

I thought back, as the car sped along, to the only other time in my life when I was locked away in a car like this. I was fifteen, at my cousin's wedding. This was early on in my partying career, so I didn't really know how to handle the rum and Cokes the cute bartender kept slipping to me all throughout cocktail hour. I shattered my glass on the dance floor during the Cupid Shuffle; I ripped my tights. In short, I was an embarrassing, sloppy mess. My dad said we had to go home, but Alanna refused. *I'm not letting her ruin my good time*, she said. So my dad dragged me out to the car, threw me in the back seat, and child-locked me in. I tried to kick out the window, but it was tempered glass, and all I managed to do was make a spiderwebbing crack. Later, when they came out to the car, they discovered me asleep in my own puke. The smell didn't leave the car for weeks, not even after I cleaned it up as punishment, not even after I paid for a new window and a professional car shampoo with my own money. I still remember how Alanna, who was a little wine-buzzed herself, took it all in—the cracked window, the masticated chicken breast and scalloped potatoes sprayed all over the back seat, and me, makeup dripping, bra strap slipping down my shoulder. Maybe she thought I was still passed out, that I couldn't hear what she said next to my dad: *I'm sorry, Jim, but you know what? On days like this, I'm glad she's not my real daughter.*

And now here I was again, a year and half later, locked away in a car for my bad behavior. And my physical response was the same. This Mary Pat person was at the ready, barf bag snapped open and passed back to me right in time. Let's just say that, coming back up, the seventeen-year-aged Bordeaux was no longer *incroyable*. Once it had finished spewing out of me, she took the bag, tied it neatly shut, and placed it on the floor between her feet in what was surely the most expensive bag of vomit ever regurgitated. She handed me a tissue to wipe my streaming eyes and an Altoid to clear out the heinous taste in my mouth. Biting down on the mint, I thought to myself that if she tried to do something like reach back, squeeze my hand, and tell me it was all going to be okay, I would knock her the fuck out. But she was a pro. She understood that with new captures, it's best to keep interaction at a minimum. I could kick and thrash as much as I wanted, but it would only be performative, an exercise in protest. She had all the power, and I had none: there was no escaping, and we both knew it.

So after handing me another tissue, Mary Pat turned back to look straight ahead at the road, talked softly to the driver, and left me alone to cry and scream and carry on as if I weren't there at all.

When I'd finally worn myself out, I put my head against the cold window and watched Chicago, the city of my whole life, drain into the distance like a bloodletting. Whatever Xander's mom took to regulate her feelings must have been some strong stuff, stronger even than fear, stronger than rage, because even though I didn't mean to, I eventually passed out again.

I didn't wake up until many hours later. We were pulling into a round gravel driveway before a series of low-slung wooden buildings with thick wilderness pressing in on all sides. I was made to understand that this was where I lived now. The sun was up, and the sky was an obscene, cloudless blue. There was something snappy and crisp about the air; it had a freshness about it that felt hostile and vaguely foreign. I didn't know what time it was, or how long we'd been driving, or even what state I was in. I reached for my phone in order to answer all these questions, but Mary Pat informed me, in an unctuous voice not unlike a funeral director's, that it had been confiscated.

"Once we get you settled in," she said, handing me a cold bottle of water, "we can talk about ways for you to earn back some tech privileges."

As I chugged the water, I thought of Xander throwing a tantrum about being kicked off his phone plan. I wondered what he would do if his father took away his actual *phone*. And his home. And his life.

"I don't even know where I am," I croaked, my voice hoarse from screaming. "You can't do this. I don't even know where I *am*."

"You're in east-central Minnesota, Mia. And you're safe. If there's anything else you want to know, all you need to do is ask."

But as she led me up the path toward the main building, with the two transport meatheads hulking behind me, the only person I had a question for was my dad. *Don't you remember what you said to me at Mom's funeral?* I mean, I was three, and *I* still remembered. In fact, it was the only thing I remembered from that day at all. Rain drumming the roof of the hired car as it crawled to the cemetery behind the yellow taillights of the hearse that carried her body. Him turning to me with his dark suit and puffy eyes and squeaky black shoes. Holding both of my hands in his. Saying: *Mia. It's just you and me now. And I will never, ever let you go.*

7

MARY PAT SHOWS ME to a seat in her office while she goes to get my paperwork. When she leaves, she takes along her letter opener and her marble paperweight—"Just out of an abundance of caution," she says with a mild smile—and locks the door from the outside. As I wait for her to come back, too shell-shocked to feel the full extent of my hangover, I pick up a glossy brochure from a pile on her desk. On the cover is a picture of three girls with their arms thrown around each other: one black, one white, one Asian, all gorgeous. They are sitting together on a giant log while a picturesque sunset lights up the pine trees behind them. They are each smiling these ridiculous big-toothed grins that are obviously meant to assuage the fears of prospective parents who are having doubts about sending their daughters away to a prison camp in the middle of nowhere. *Not only have we been thoroughly brainwashed into compliance*, the girls on the log seem to be saying, *but we've had fun doing it!*

I open the pamphlet and begin to read.

× × ×

**RED OAK
ACADEMY**

Parenting isn't easy.
But it should never be this hard.
Let us help.

Welcome to Red Oak Academy, a therapeutic boarding school for troubled teenage girls. We are a fully accredited high school located on ten beautiful wooded acres in east-central Minnesota, just outside the Rum River State Forest—a one-of-a-kind facility that combines the latest in therapeutic pedagogy with the ancient healing qualities of Mother Nature. Our program is designed to help your daughter find her way back to the life she was meant to lead and the person she was meant to be. Our pledge is that when we return your daughter to you after her program has reached maturation, she will be like the red oak for which our school is named, and by which our school is surrounded, growing straight and tall and proud in the forest of her life.

Our treatment approach is distinctly holistic and tailored to each individual student's needs. Unlike some more traditional therapeutic schools, we do not *engage in practices*

*that are rooted in patriarchal, militaristic systems—e.g.,
uniforms, honor codes, "levels," traditional academic grades,
etc. We believe this holistic, individualized approach is what
distinguishes us from other therapeutic boarding programs.
In this spirit, please be aware of what we are* NOT:

   A wilderness program

   A drug rehabilitation facility

   A mental health facility

   A boot camp

   A lockdown facility

This last bullet point is sort of a comfort. If it's not a lockdown facility, does that mean I can leave whenever I want? But when I look at the locked door before me, or out the window behind me, with its thick wall of forest on every side, filled with trees growing *straight and tall and proud*,[5] I wonder where it would be that I could even go.

Who Is a Red Oak Girl?

She is your *daughter: a smart, loving young woman,
between the ages of thirteen and eighteen, who has simply lost
her way. She may be:*

   Making poor and dangerous choices

   Acting entitled, selfish, or detached

   Manipulative

   Lying

---

[5] BARFFFFFFF

Sneaking out
Rebellious
Depressed
Withdrawn
Self-destructive
Narcissistic
Histrionic
Eating-disordered
Violent
Promiscuous
Academically unmotivated
*Using/abusing drugs and/or alcohol beyond
the experimental stage*
Experiencing grief and/or trauma
Experiencing attachment struggles
Engaging in school refusal
Unable to adhere to rules or limits
Unable to regulate her moods
Expressing suicidal ideation
Self-harming
Easily influenced by others; lacking a solid sense of self
Oppositional
Fire-starting

Huh.

Like, okay.

I admit: *some* of these apply to me. I make poor and

dangerous choices. I manipulate, I rebel, I'm promiscuous, I'm defiant, I use/abuse drugs and/or alcohol beyond the experimental stage, I'm academically unmotivated, and while technically speaking I am *able* to adhere to rules and limits, I usually choose not to. But honestly, that also probably describes a good chunk of the people I hang out with. I mean, look at Xander! He's a burnout, a thief of rare aged wines, a man whore, and a *drug dealer.* So why am *I* the one who got sent away?

And what about this other stuff?

Suicidal ideation?

Self-harming?

Fire-starting???

I mean, even if I admit that I'm bad, I'm not, like, *arsonist* bad. I'm not hurting-myself-and-others bad (Alanna's nose doesn't count; that was *one time*, and if you'd heard what she said to me, you would agree that she completely deserved it).

I look around Mary Pat's office with its wood-paneled walls, its folksy tchotchkes lining the bookcases, its cozy braided rug, its framed oil paintings of ducks. The place looks like some kind of sinister, alt-universe Cracker Barrel. And my dad thinks *this* is the kind of place I belong, with *these* kinds of people? As I wait for Mary Pat to come back, an awful image forms in my head: of him and Alanna sitting late at night at the kitchen table, heads pressed together, pens in hand. I picture them going through this list and ticking off box after box, each checkmark an affirmation that the only solution they have left is to farm me out to a band of psychology-degree-wielding, non-militaristic, non-patriarchal strangers. And with each checked box, even though they won't admit it—even to each other—both of them feel a growing sense of excitement. With me no longer in the picture, they can finally be who *they're* meant to be, the Dempseys: just a mom, a dad, and their two adorable and fully biological children. Without me around, they can finally be a normal family. A *nuclear family*, as they say, but with its nuclear piece, which has threatened for years to blow them all to pieces, finally defused for good.

8

AFTER MARY PAT HAS handed me a clear plastic backpack filled with a couple notebooks,[6] a Red Oak student handbook, and my small purple duffel bag from home, filled with clothes Alanna must have packed and shipped in advance of my ambush, she leads me to a windowless cinder-block room down the hall from her office. The floor is concrete, the track lighting is harsh yellow, and there's nothing in the rectangular space except for two chairs and a long table with a plastic bin on it, the kind you see at airport security where you have to put your keys and jacket. There are two women sitting in the chairs. The one with long flat-ironed hair is tall and mom-like, in her Dansko clogs, craft fair earrings, and blue scrubs. The other is short and shapeless, young enough to still have acne, with unevenly applied eyeliner, a messy bun tied at the top of her head, and a wavy blood-colored line at her hairline where her drugstore dye has bled into her scalp. She's wearing a T-shirt that reads

---

[6] The soft-bound composition kind and not the spiral kind; spiral notebook wire could be repurposed as a weapon or self-harm tool.

RED OAK STAFF across the front.

"Mia," says Mary Pat, "let me introduce you to Melanie, our school nurse practitioner, and Dee, our assistant team leader."

Both women stand to greet me; I look past them like they aren't even there.

"Nurse Melanie is going to weigh you and take your vitals, and then I'm going to do a quick search of your person."

My *person*? I don't actually hate her weirdly formal choice of words. It dissociates me from my body—my body is my person, and I'm me. Two separate things: and these bitches can only search one of them.

When I go to step onto the scale, Nurse Melanie stops me.

"If you don't mind, Mia," she says, "I'd ask that you turn around and step up backward."

"Why?"

"Some of our girls have body dysmorphia and problematic eating patterns, so we have a policy of keeping students' weight confidential."

"Well, *I* don't have an eating disorder."

"Standard intake procedure, honey."

Now I'm more annoyed that she just called me *honey*. I sigh, turn around, step backward onto the scale, and wait for her to record my weight. Then she takes my blood pressure and listens to my heartbeat, recording all my results in her laptop.

"I'll ask you to remove your clothes now," Mary Pat says, as she pulls two blue rubber gloves from a disposable packet on the table.

"Wait. You're going to *strip*-search me?"

"Again, this is standard intake procedure."

"Fuck that. I opt out of standard intake procedure."

Mary Pat smiles at me with the unruffled American-heartland efficiency that I've already come to loathe. "Mia, if you refuse to cooperate, then we'll have to hold you down and remove your clothes forcibly. But I'd really like to avoid that, if at all possible. That kind of physical interaction can be very triggering for some of our girls."

I stand in the middle of the well-lit room, looking back and forth between these three women. I know I haven't exactly led a life of dignity these last few years, but still, this feels egregious. At least when I'm taking off my clothes for some-body, they're taking off their clothes, too. Plus, the room is usually dark.

"Now go on ahead and remove your clothes, please, and place them in the bin. This won't take more than a minute."

Nurse Melanie smiles at me and nods gently. Dee waits, watching me. I notice the thickness of her arms, the sturdi-ness of her short, bowed legs. Her face is impassive, but there is a certain mean energy in her eyes, a challenge. She *wants* me to fight this. She wants to put her hands on me, display her dominance. I realize that I hate her. It feels good. One of my little rules of life is that if you're ever in a situation where you're feeling vulnerable, the best thing to do is pick out somebody to hate. Hate is an uncomplicated emotion. It will give you something to latch on to, clean out your mind and strip you down to the animal that you are, reminding you that, as an animal, you have only one real job to accomplish, which is to survive.

I stare Dee down as I unbutton my jeans.

I'm still wearing Xander's favorite bra—the black lacy one with the sheer band and the straps that dig into my shoulders. He bought it for me, which is why it's the completely wrong size—he was unaware that bra sizes had numbers *and* letters. I never wear it except when I know I'm going to be seeing him. As I unhook it and toss it into the bin, even my humiliation can't prevent me from feeling the physical sensation of relief every girl experiences when she takes off an ill-fitting undergarment for the day. I hope that Alanna, in her haste to get rid of me, at least remembered to pack me a sports bra.

I pull down my underwear quickly, squeeze it into a ball, and toss it into the bin. I stare up at the particleboard ceiling, blinking carefully because I'm afraid, suddenly, that I might cry. Goose bumps prick my skin as Mary Pat skims my shoulders and waist with her gloved hands.

"Almost done," I hear her say. "You're doing just fine, Mia. Now, bend over, please, and place your hands on the floor."

I can feel Dee watching me, feel the imbalance of power that her smirk implies, as I touch my palms to the concrete. I tell myself again that my body is just a body and the me of who I am is something they can't see or touch. *If you cry right now*, I think to myself as Mary Pat's gloved fingers begin to probe me, *then they'll see you. If you let them see you, you're letting them win.*

They even make me squat to make sure I didn't smuggle in anything up my vagina, like I'm some desperate drug mule. When I comply, Mary Pat and Dee and Nurse Melanie all stand there looking at the floor, as if they expect a gun to fall out or something. When nothing does, I swear Dee almost looks disappointed.

I hurry to put my clothes back on, thinking this is finally over, but then Mary Pat informs me that they need to make some "stylistic changes" to my *person* in order to make me dress code compliant. Nurse Melanie sits me down in one of the chairs and, with an apologetic murmur, snips off the colored ends of my hair.[7] I watch the lavender curls sift to the floor, thinking of the day I bleached them with Eve, my sort-of friend, in the flickering basement light of her mom's boyfriend's apartment, while washing machines hummed and shook all around us like rows of giant hatching eggs.

---

[7] Red Oak Academy student handbook section 8.3: personal grooming—hair: hair must be kept no more than two shades lighter or darker than student's natural color.

Next, they declaw me, cutting down my nails nearly to the quick.[8] Then they take out my tongue piercing.[9] Mary Pat and Dee hold me down by the shoulders while Nurse Melanie, with another murmured *honey* and a gentleness that somehow still feels ruthless, forces open my mouth. Working quickly, as if she does this all the time, and I suppose she probably does, she unscrews the ball at the top and slips out the bar from the bottom. I've had this bar in since sophomore year, and without it, my mouth feels weirdly empty. I run my denuded tongue against the roof of my mouth, and the hole in the flesh feels the way it used to when I was a little kid and lost a tooth. I want to spit in their faces, but the hangover and the fear have dried up my saliva.

The last and final step is a pee test. They let me do this alone and with the door closed, in a small bathroom next to the intake room, but they make me shout-count the whole time I'm in there, I guess so they know I'm not climbing up on the toilet and hoisting myself out through the latch

---

[8] Red Oak Academy student handbook section 8.4: personal grooming—nails: finger and toenails must be kept short and neatly trimmed. Synthetic tips, decals, and other nail design products are not permitted. Nail polish is permitted at the discretion of staff and must be certified organic and "3-free" (nontoxic and containing no toluene, DBP, or formaldehyde). Nail polish may only be applied under staff supervision.

[9] Red Oak Academy student handbook section 9.4: dress code—jewelry: clasped metal items designed to be worn around the neck and wrist are not permitted. Soft items (scapulars, woven friendship bracelets, scrunchies, etc.) are permitted at the discretion of staff. A maximum of two earrings per ear are permitted. Piercings are restricted to the earlobe and *only* the earlobe.

window and running off into the forest.

"Okay!" Mary Pat says as I hand over the warm cup filled with bright yellow hangover pee. "The unpleasant stuff is over now. What do you say we go meet your new classmates?"

9

THE FIRST GIRL I MEET is my roommate, Madison, a grinning lump of insecurity dressed head to toe in bougie-brand yoga clothes who has been tasked with showing me our room and then walking me down to the cafeteria for lunch.

My old high school was filled with girls like her: girls who dress and think strictly in pastels, girls with no chill and no spine. Girls from one of those two-golden-retrievers families, one of those matching-turtlenecks-on-the-holiday-card families, the dumbest but hardest-working student in your honors class.

She's pretty, I guess: with pink skin, silky yellow curls, and the buggy, wet blue eyes of a Victorian china doll that blink at me from behind a pair of chunky Kate Spade glasses. But it's a very temporary kind of pretty. Even though she can't be more than sixteen or seventeen, I can see that it's already fading. In a few years, her ass will melt from round to wide, her chin will soften and then multiply, her hair will turn prematurely gray and she'll never find a colorist who can quite restore that sunny shade of blond. I only need to take one look at her to know which box *she* ticks.

Easily influenced by others; lacking a solid sense of self.

I can picture exactly how it all went down: how her parents went out of town, leaving her in charge, with a warning that they trusted her. And she *meant* to do everything right, but then some popular boy flirted with her a little, convinced her to have a tiny little get-together—just a few friends! They'd play Scrabble!

Okay, she'd said, smiling at him gummily, *but seriously Tyler, just a few people.*

Of course, Madison, he'd soothed. Then he'd patted her on her pretty yellow head, turned around, whipped out his phone and invited every person he'd ever met. The mob descended across Madison's wide green lawn, poured into the marble foyer, and destroyed everything in sight with the casual venom reserved for unpopular girls who are dumb enough to think they can buy approval by throwing parties. Was a beloved family heirloom shattered/stolen/pissed on? Was the family parrot defeathered? Did someone drown in the in-ground pool? Whatever it was, Madison's parents thought they could bury it by sending her here, and she went willingly, her tail tucked between her pigeon-toed legs, to work on her *sense of self.*

I'm so pleased with my psychological analysis of Madison's character that it takes me a moment to notice her hands.

I'll admit, they throw me off.

Because, well, they are horrifying.

Raw and meaty, with strips of skin around her cuticles and fingertips gnawed and peeled back to the bloody underlayer. You can't really even describe it as nail biting. It's more like self-cannibalization. It isn't restricted to the fingers, either. Along the thick part of her palms, there are red sores that at first I think must be eczema until I notice her methodically gnawing on the skin there, too, like a wild animal with its leg caught in a trap.

"Doesn't that *hurt*?"

"What?" She drops her hand from her mouth sheepishly. A piece of her own skin hangs from her bottom lip. "I bite my nails."

"No, you *eat* your *hands*."

"Whatever! It's just a bad habit. I have a thing with impulse control, especially when I'm stressed. I've been super nervous the last couple days because they told me I was getting a new roommate—you!"

She smiles at me with such urgent goodwill that I half expect her to throw her arms around me, and maybe she would have, except for the fact that, brochure of girls hugging on a log notwithstanding, in actuality we are not allowed to touch each other under any circumstances.[10]

---

[10] Red Oak Academy student handbook section 4.9: on-campus rules—personal conduct: Many of our girls come to us with boundary issues. While at Red Oak, students will learn to increase their understanding and respect for the personal space of themselves and others. To that end, students must maintain a six-inch separation between themselves and their peers at all times. No cuddling, hugging, hand-holding, high-fiving, lap sitting, tickling, or other forms of intentional physical contact are permitted.

x x x

The lunchroom looks like a regular school cafeteria, except that its five small tables only seat about twenty kids, max, and there are no boys and out the huge picture windows there is no parking lot or football field, just wilderness, flamingly beautiful in its fall colors.

As we approach the counter, a big-breasted lunch lady in a Minnesota Vikings T-shirt smiles and greets us—both of us, even though it's only my first day and I've never even met her—by name. *Hi, Madison! Hi, Mia!* I look down at what she's dumped onto my tray: plain peanut butter on white bread. Unripened pear. Orange Jell-O.

Prison food.

We move to the beverage station. There is no pop or coffee—"caffeine is an addictive substance!" Madison explains sunnily—only orange juice, milk, or water, and these tiny little plastic cups, like we're in preschool.

"Is that why you're here?" I watch as Madison pours herself three cups of OJ. "Because of your thing with impulse control?"

"Pretty much."

"Bullshit!"

A tall skinny girl with a long tangle of black hair and a sun-starved olive complexion bangs her tray down next to us. She's wearing Docs and a sundress made of a thin yellow fabric that shows her nipples. She must be freezing—it's mid-October and we're in Minnesota—and her bare, hairy arms bristle with goose bumps.

"Shut up, Vera." Madison bites into her sandwich.

Vera has small, straight teeth and a sharp, zit-spackled face, divided down the middle by a large beaky nose. With those features, it feels like she should be ugly, but when you put them all together, somehow, like a cubist painting, it sums up into something beautiful. She smells like men's Old Spice and BO and unwashed hair, and despite my vow to hate everyone and everything at Red Oak Academy, I like her immediately.

"Be honest, Madison," she says, winking at me. "Hold yourself accountable. The *real* reason you're here is because you're a stalker."

Madison sighs. "For the millionth time, I'm not a *stalker*. I went through a bad *breakup*."

"Lots of people go through bad breakups. Few people decide to make a homemade pipe bomb and stick it under their ex-girlfriend's car." Vera unpeels the crust from her sandwich bread in one long piece, like skinning a fish, and discards it onto the corner of her tray. "Luckily," she explains to me, "this is Madison we're talking about, so of course the bomb didn't work right. When it exploded, all it did was blow out a tire, but the poor chick happened to be driving on the freeway, so she crashed into the median and broke her arm and like three ribs."

"Yeah, which was exactly what I *intended*. I only meant to scare her. If I had really wanted to *kill* her, I would have constructed the stupid bomb with steel, which has a much higher concussive force than plastic. It's not like I learned *nothing* in those five summers of STEM camp my parents forced me into. *Jeez*."

"Come on now, Madison," says another girl with flawless dark skin and black braids pushed back from her face with a wide pink headband, as she slides in next to Vera. "You know what Mary Pat says: 'Only by owning our actions can we begin to reconcile them.'"

"Yeah," Madison snaps, "like you guys are all so *perfect*."

"No need to raise your voice, dear," the girl teases, her Southern drawl morphing into a clipped, earnest Midwestern accent that's a dead ringer for Mary Pat. "You know what I always say: 'Anger is a secondhand emotion.'"

Madison rolls her big wet eyes and adjusts her glasses. She puts her sandwich back on her tray to resume eating her hand instead.

"I'm Trinity." The girl with the headband is looking me over now. "Who are *you*?"

"Mia."

"Where you from?"

"Chicago."

"They take your phone yet?"

I nod.

"*Dammit.*"

"Did you really think they'd forget something like that?" asks Madison. "That's like 'standard intake procedure.'"

"Ugh," I say. "If I have to hear that phrase *one* more time."

"They search your coochie?"

I nod, annoyed at myself for the involuntary flare of heat in my face.

"You can thank this one for that." Trinity jabs a thumb in Vera's direction. "The squat search didn't used to be part of the deal until she decided to sneak in a bottle of airplane vodka up her vajayjay last semester."

"That's why they call it nature's pocket," Vera says cheerfully.

Madison looks at me, scrunching up her face in disgust. "And they think *I'm* the freak."

"For real, though," Trinity says, looking around the table. "I *need* to get my hands on somebody's phone. I am in *serious* need of access to my platforms."

"You see, Mia," Vera explains, "Trinity had over a hundred thousand Instagram followers when her parents sent her here."

"I was an influencer," Trinity says proudly. "I was making *money*. But I haven't been able to post content in months. Without content, I have no personal brand. And without personal branding, I don't have a *chance*."

Vera laughs, a husky, windblown snicker that sends goose

bumps threading up my own skin. "If a tree falls in the forest and nobody Boomerangs it and adds it to their story, did it really even happen?"

"Trin," says Madison, pulling her hand away from her face as a thread of drool extends, glistening like a spider's web, "most of your followers were old perverts who just liked ogling those pictures of you so you could star in their gross fantasies. Not to sound judgy or anything, but that would make me feel so, like, *violated*."

"Oh, shut up, Madison. One time I was on the train, wearing baggy sweats, no makeup, every *inch* of my body covered, and some fool whipped his dick out at me anyway. There are certain kinds of men, girls our age give them nasty thoughts just by being *alive*. So if you can't control other people's fantasies, why not at least make money off them?"

"*I* get that logic," says Vera. "Too bad your mom didn't."

"She's super Christian," Madison explains.

"*And* a United States congresswoman," adds Vera.

"*Former* United States congresswoman," Madison corrects her. "She lost her reelection last year. People figured, if she couldn't control her daughter, how could she control, like, the economy or whatever?"

Trinity just yawns. She doesn't look sorry.

"Anyway, you'll get used to it, not having a phone," Vera says to me. "I barely even remember how to take a selfie. Or why someone would *want* to take a selfie. I'm like a pioneer woman. Or a cult wife. Or a fucking astronaut. I don't live in the world anymore—I live in Red Oak."

"How long have you been here?" I ask.

"Almost two years."

"Two *years*?"

I thought maybe my dad and Alanna would stick me here for a couple weeks, thirty days at the absolute most. Just long enough to teach me a lesson. It hadn't even occurred to me until now that I could be stuck here for the rest of high school. They would never do that to me, though. Would they? Well, Dad wouldn't. But Alanna . . . I start to feel that tingling sensation in the center of my chest, the first whispering tendrils of a panic attack. If I don't get in front of this, the tingling can turn quickly into a drowning feeling, like someone's just pulled a plastic bag over my head and is starting to tie it up tightly. I want a narcotic intervention. Like, now. But since my last psychiatrist discontinued all my prescription meds due to my "addictive personality," and a strip search, a confiscated phone, and several hundred miles of highway stand between me and one of Xander's little orange pills, I put a hand up to my throat and breathe deeply through my nose the way she taught me. It's better than nothing, I guess.

"Don't worry, Mia." Madison's eyes behind her glasses are filled with roommately concern. "Most people don't stay that long. Vera's a special case."

I nod gratefully and breathe out.

"Yeah, it's been a minute." Vera kicks a long stubbly leg up onto our lunch table and points to her scuffed Docs. "I've completely lost touch with contemporary culture. Are these even cool anymore?"

"Docs never *were* cool, in my world," says Trinity. She sighs. "I miss my Louboutins."[11]

"Oh, Trinity," Vera says. "It's so sad how you succumb to toxic princess culture, not to mention the hegemonic structures that equalize femininity with walking around on torturous stilts. Not to *mention* the fact that Louboutins, despite their absurd price tag, are just so tragically basic."

"Only white girls can be basic. We've been over this."

"I disagree," Madison begins. "There was this one girl at my old school—"

"Shut up, Madison," the other two say in unison, and I feel like I can breathe again, because even though (if the *Who Is a Red Oak Girl?* list is any indication) these girls are all insane, the way they bicker with each other feels reassuringly normal.

"My *point*," Vera says, kicking her feet back to the floor, "is that *I* prefer, whenever possible, to be comfortable." She begins sawing at her pear with a plastic knife. I see Dee, the Red Oak equivalent of a lunch monitor, standing in the

---

[11] Red Oak Academy student handbook section 9.1: dress code—footwear: students must wear shoes at all times when they are on school grounds outside of their dormitories. Shoes must be closed-toed, with a heel no higher than one and a half inches, and must be worn with socks and/or unripped tights.

middle of the room and holding a clipboard. I notice that she doesn't take her eyes off us until Vera puts down her knife.

"So if two years isn't the standard," I say, trying to sound casual as the rhythm of my heartbeat starts to even out, "what is?"

"Every girl comes to us exhibiting her own unique battery of issues," explains Trinity, and I can't tell if she's still making fun of Mary Pat or if Red Oak girls are so therapized that this is just how they talk. "And every girl's treatment plan and LOS[12] varies. Not sure if you heard, but we do not adhere to patriarchal, militaristic methods, which means that your release date will be soft and negotiable, depending on how well Mary Pat and your individual counselor think you're doing the emotional work."

"My individual counselor?"

"Yeah, there's three of them. Everybody gets assigned one. They meet with you two times a week and they're like your point person here. Your counselor pretty much holds the key to your exit. Lemme see your schedule, and we can see who you've got."

I produce the printout Mary Pat gave me at intake, and Trinity points to a name in the top right-hand corner of the folded paper. *St. John, Dr. Vivian.*

"Lucky." Madison pouts. "I've got Carolyn, and Carolyn sort of sucks."

---

[12] LOS = length of stay

"And I've got Bad Breath Brit," Trin says, with an epic eye roll. "You're lucky, Mia. People *love* Vivian."

"And those people," Vera says, "suffer from Stockholm syndrome." She forks a slice of pear, nibbles off a tiny corner of flesh, and looks at me. "I've got Vivian, too. Our sessions are painfully pointless—don't expect miracles. And anyway, it doesn't even matter who you've got, because what an LOS really comes down to is how fucked up you actually are. So the question is: Are you someone like me, who is *truly* and incorrigibly bad? Or are you simply a girl who isn't 'good,' with parents who don't know how to deal, like Trinity here?"

"I may have been an Instagram porn star," Trinity says, sitting up straight and primly lacing her fingers together, "but I'm still a virgin who loves Jesus."

"So which one are you?" Madison looks at me eagerly. "Bad, or just not good?"

"No, let *us* figure it out," Vera says before I can answer. "It's more fun that way! The first thing we need to know is why you're here. You didn't threaten to shoot up your school, did you?"

"Nah," says Trinity. "She doesn't look like the violent type. I say drugs."

"Meth? No—that's not really a Chicago thing. It'd be coke. Or some sort of opioid."

"You banged your teacher."

"Or your best friend's daddy."

"Or your best friend's mom?"

"Did you steal a car? And then crash it through the front window of a Build-A-Bear Workshop?"

"Shut *up*, Madison. That was Olivia who did that. The same thing isn't going to happen twice."

"Are you gang affiliated?"

"Are you a kleptomaniac?"

"Are you a huge slut?"

"She *definitely* associates with an unhealthy peer group."

"I'm telling y'all, it's drugs. But which *ones*?"

"Cat? Horse? Amy?"

"Molly? White Girl? China Girl?"

"Sizzurp? Special K? Oxy? O Bombs?"

"Adderall? Ritalin? Vicadin? Demerol?"

"Weed? Wine? Whippits?"

"Dusting?"

"Hold up." Trinity lifts a hand, and her nails are beautiful—just short enough to be handbook compliant, but perfectly filed and painted an impeccable, glossy pink. They are in every way the opposite of Madison's chewed night-mares, and I wonder how she maintains them in the midst of this deranged Girl Scout camp. "What in the name of the Lord is *dusting*?"

"You know those cans of air that you use to spray out the dust from between your keyboard keys?" says Vera. "People huff them."

"That's a thing?"

"Sure."

"I didn't think Upper East Side girls fucked with that kind of nonsense."

"I'm from the Upper *West* Side, first of all," sniffs Vera. "And second of all, we don't. That shit's *toxic*. If it doesn't straight-up kill you the first time you try it, which it very well might, it gives you like a ten-second high that turns you into some foaming, inchoate vegetable. What's fun about that? Plus, it's trashy. I don't want to have to go to, like, OfficeMax to get my fix."

Trinity starts to retort, but I cut her off.

"I don't *dust*, okay? I don't do practically any of the stuff you guys just listed. The only reason I'm here is because my stepmom is a bitch and she didn't want to deal with me anymore."

The three of them exchange a look before bursting into gales of derisive laughter.

"*What?*"

"That is *classic* first-day talk," Vera says, collapsing back in her chair and laughing horsily. "*The whole world is against me and I did nothing wrong!*"

I'm about to turn it around on Vera, ask her what *she* did to get here, but then she reaches up to brush a hank of black hair from her face and that's when I see the ridged white mounds of scar tissue that jag across the inside of her delicate wrist, and other scars, smaller but numerous, slicing up her thin forearm, methodical and self-inflicted. I feel a grim sort of satisfaction then, because my secrets are all on the inside, which means I can guard them for as long as I want.

10

MY SECOND NIGHT, I'm awoken by thunder. Outside, the rain is lashing down, hissing against the wall of trees that surround campus. I'm lying on my back, listening to the sound, and to Madison's shallow, even breathing in the bunk above me.

Eventually I get up, my feet cold on the creaking tiles, and tiptoe over to the window. I try to push it open, but it only goes up a few inches before locking in place, to prevent anyone from trying to get in or out, I guess.

But I'm not trying to run away.

I'm just trying to feel the rain on my face, that inside-outside feeling, the way I used to do when I was a kid.

When I was five, my dad bought me this princess bed, with a canopy and everything—the kind of indulgent gift a widowed man buys for his motherless daughter—and he set it up right beneath my bedroom window. I used to lay there at night with the blankets pulled up to my chin and the nighttime rain misting through the screen, dappling my face. And when it got to be too cold or too wet, I'd slam the window shut and burrow down under the covers, overcome with this delicious feeling of safety, with the rain pattering outside and a sturdy roof over my head and my dad alive and snoring across the hall.

When I got older, that window became my passage into the night, my portal for sneaking out, because I no longer wanted to be safe, it was no longer enough just to taste the rain; I wanted to feel the water over my whole body.

My dad, thinking he could solve the problem by taking away my privacy, got out his wrench and took my bedroom door off its hinges. And his tactic worked, kind of. I did stop sneaking out.

Instead, I just started leaving. Right out the front door, right in front of their faces, whenever I wanted to. Which didn't feel good, not at all. But it still felt like a victory.

11

STARTING TODAY, I'm going to be forced to meet with Vivian St. John, PhD, for one hour every Monday and Wednesday afternoon until I get out of here. She tells me, at my first appointment in her tiny office in the back of the admin building, that she was born and raised here in Onamia. She says she's half white, half Ojibwe, then points out at the stream running past—so close I can hear its burbling even with the window closed—and tells me that her father's people have lived on Red Oak land for over five centuries.

"Well, no offense to your father's people," I say, "but this place sucks."

"Most of our girls think that, at least at first." She has still-black hair, good skin, and two deep dimples in the middle of her cheeks. You can tell that she was pretty before she got old. "I bet you have a lot of questions for me."

"Just one, actually. When the fuck am I getting out of here?"

"The journey is the important thing here, Mia. Not the destination."

"Huh. I think I read that once on a decorative poster. It

was in the home decor aisle at Michaels, right next to the Live Laugh Love signs."

"You know, Mia, your feelings of anger are perfectly normal. I'd be more concerned about you if you *weren't* furious at your parents for sending you to Red Oak. It's a drastic step, and one that can be hard to reconcile. But for most girls, that anger fades with time, and—"

"Let me guess—then the brainwashing begins, and two years later you'll send me home, normal and happy and emotionally lobotomized?"

"Ha! I won't say Red Oak is perfect. We might have forcibly removed your tongue piercing, Mia, but we're not going to forcibly remove your prefrontal cortex. Even if we *were* a medical facility, which we're not, a lobotomy hasn't been performed in the United States since the 1970s. And thank goodness for that, because the procedure is as close as human beings have ever come to the surgical murder of a soul—and, no surprise, the large majority of them were performed on women. You see, even though we've gotten better about it, our society has never quite known how to deal with a woman who refuses to toe the line. Which is partially why schools like Red Oak exist."

I slump back in my chair. I was wondering what kind of therapist Vivian was going to be, and now I know: the kind that loves to hear herself talk.

"Now, in terms of our ability to make you 'normal,' the idea of normalcy varies so wildly from culture to culture and person to person that there's no actual benchmark that could ever be useful. So in some sense, everybody's normal and nobody's normal. As for happiness, of all the things Western culture has gotten wrong, this obsession with happiness might be the silliest. Trying to teach someone to be happy is about as effective as trying to cut water with scissors."

"I thought we weren't allowed to have scissors here."

"I'm glad to see you've read the school handbook. Your dad told me you love to read." She taps her pen against her notepad. "What's your favorite novel?"

"*Moby-Dick.*"

"Wow. That's a big one." She arches an eyebrow at me. "Are you just saying that to impress me?"

"Why would I try to impress you when I don't give a shit about you?"

My insult glances off her without so much as a twitch.

"What do you like best about *Moby-Dick*?"

"Have you read it?"

"Nah. I spent my school years reading nothing but dead white men. Now I read what *I* want."

"Well, Melville was a genius. *He* definitely had some opinions on whiteness, that's for sure."

"Is that so?"

I'm expecting her to test me now, to ask me what some of those opinions were so that I can launch into a long disquisition about the whiteness of the whale that will leave her feeling both impressed and intellectually inferior, but instead she pivots the conversation completely.

"You ever read any Native lit? Louise Erdrich? Tommy Orange? Layli Long Soldier? Joy Harjo?"

I don't answer her. I won't give her the satisfaction of knowing that I haven't read those authors. If she thinks that makes me ignorant, that's her business.

"We have a wonderful little library here on campus, just behind Conifer House. Have you gotten the chance to check it out yet?"

"You mean between group chat and chores and classes and mandatory lights-out at nine o'clock? No, I haven't."

"Well, the next time you *do* get some free time, I think you'd like it there. It's always unlocked, even at night—like a church. It's the only place on campus, other than the walking trails, that you can go without permission during designated constructive relaxation hours."

This interests me—slightly—but does this woman really expect me to demonstrate excitement about the prospect of being allowed to go sit by myself in a library? Me, who was once the proud owner of a fake ID so authentic it had worked everywhere, not just the skeevy strip mall liquor stores but in Whole fucking Foods itself? Is this how pathetic my life has now become? So instead I just shrug and stare out the window at the moving stream.

× × ×

It isn't until forty minutes later, when I'm walking out of our session, the main two topics of which are literature and lobotomies, that I realize Vivian didn't ask me one question about my dad or Alanna; Xander or my other boyfriends; my failing grades or my drinking or drugging or *what happened to my mother*. I wonder whether she's trying to pull some *Good Will Hunting* shit on me, or whether she's just dumb. I decide it's the latter. Who cares if she's got a PhD diploma from some fancy East Coast school hanging on her wall? I would easily be able to get into any of those Ivy League colleges, too—if I could just get the chance to go back to freshman year and do everything all over again, differently.

12

ALL MY CLASSES HERE except English are independent studies. This means that you go into a classroom and sit in front of a computer that's programmed to block any website that isn't a part of your personally tailored distance-learning curriculum. Math is the only period of the day that all the girls from my dorm, Birchwood House, are together, so it's a no-brainer as to where I'm going to sit.

On Friday, the last day of my first week, Vera and I are doing more gossiping than problem-solving while across the room Ms. Gina squints at the master computer, pretending like she's checking our work when really we can all tell she's just scrolling through social media.

"So you're from Manhattan," I say to her. "Does that mean you're rich?"

"Oh, you mean you haven't heard my joke yet?"

"Uh—no?"

"What's the difference between a troubled teen and an at-risk youth?"

"No clue."

"Money." She laughs, and submits a wrong answer on her precalc exercise. The computer bloops at her, and she gives it the finger.

"But seriously, how could my family afford to put me up at this place for two years and counting if I wasn't disgustingly loaded? It's kind of embarrassing, actually. I have so much privilege that if I *tried* to check it, it would take up the whole bottom of the airplane. My dad comes from Bahraini oil royalty. And my mom's your prototypical Connecticut WASP. Her great-grandmother was British. Like the upper-crusty kind. Here, look." She leans down and reaches into the clear front pocket of her backpack. She hands me an antique-looking pocket watch, with the clock face on one side and a compass on the other. It looks like it's made of solid gold, and it's inlaid with all sorts of swirling floral designs.

"This was hers. Both she and it survived the sinking of the *Titanic*."

"Damn." I turn the watch over in my hands. It's as heavy and cool as a stone freshly scooped from the ocean. "So she was one of the few to make it onto an escape boat?"

"Are you kidding me? Of *course* Imogen Swift got a spot on an escape boat. She and her buds were draped in fur blankets and served champagne while all around them, the peasants thrashed and froze in the North Atlantic."

"Ladies," calls Ms. Gina, her eyes flicking up from what I can only presume is some sort of cat meme, "it better be exponential functions you two are discussing."

"I'm just showing her the formula for growth and decay," I answer, pretending to type something on Vera's keyboard. "You see, Vera," I say loudly, "$y = a(1-r)$ to the x power."

Ms. Gina, who I can already tell is lazy and doesn't actually care what we're doing as long as we do it quietly, especially on a Friday, returns to her scrolling.

"I do take some consolation in the fact that not dying on the *Titanic* seemed to really fuck my great-great-grandma Imogen up," Vera continues at a lowered volume. "She wasn't *totally* soulless apparently. She made it to New York and married some equally aristocratic dude when she got there, but for the rest of her life she suffered from 'nervous fits,' as they called them back then. Which is probably as good an explanation as any of how I inherited *my* issues. They were passed down to me from some corset-wearing snob sipping her bubbly and bobbing along in the ocean while all around her, drowning Irish children used their last breaths to scream for their mothers."

I consider this for a moment as I submit my own answer to a word problem.

"So what are you saying? That trauma is hereditary?"

"Of course it is! Living through extreme guilt or trauma: that shit alters you on a cellular level. It can be suffered by our ancestors and then bleed down into us, as hereditary as hammertoe or heart disease."

"And *that*," Trin chimes in, "is just another reason why the descendants of slaves should be entitled to reparations."

"What are reparations?"

"*Shut up, Madison*," we all yell in unison, followed by an explosion of laughter, for which we are all punished with an extra half hour of homework.

13

THAT EVENING, during constructive relaxation, I decide I need a break from all my new classmates, their bickering, their drama, their rapacious need for attention. After I've finished my homework, I take Vivian's advice and head over to the library. The building is nothing more than a tiny A-framed log cabin right at the edge of school property, with two narrow front windows and a red painted door, which, as she promised, is unlocked.

Inside, it's totally quiet, except for the autumn rain pattering on the two wide skylights overhead. Dust motes swirl around in the book-scented air. It's warm and dry, and best of all, most of the girls are playing in an interhouse Uno tournament,[13] so nobody's here but me.

At one end of the cabin, a fire burns low but steady in a black marble fireplace. I think of the fire-starter girls who go to school here and wonder why Mary Pat would flirt with disaster this way. But when I get closer, I realize that the fire is just a little flat-screen TV mounted inside the fireplace, and the screen is playing an endless loop of computerized

---

[13] This, apparently, is what constitutes a wild Friday night in this place.

flame. Which is so typical of adults: they like to give you the idea that they trust you, but when you step closer you realize it's just an illusion.

Still, it's cozy in here, with the radiators along the baseboards ticking and sighing. I walk between the narrow rows of bookcases, running my fingers along the spines, scanning the titles. One name jumps out at me because I remember Vivian mentioning it at our first session. Joy Harjo. I slip the book out from the shelf and look at the cover. Poetry. Not really my thing. It always feels so self-important: all *Look at my gorgeous words with all their indecipherable deep meanings!* Novels are what I like—the bigger the better, hence my love of *Moby-Dick*—long enough for me to get lost in. But I figure I'll give old Joy a shot, for Vivian's sake, because I've always liked doing nice things for people in ways they don't know about and will never see. I toe off my wet shoes and curl up next to the fake fire in one of the two creaky velvet chairs on the hearth, flip to a random poem, and begin to read.

Ah, ah slaps the urgent cove of ocean swimming through the slips[14]

And before I even mean to, I'm thinking about her again, the most and least important person in my life: my mother,

---

[14] "Ah, Ah," by Joy Harjo, from How We Became Human: New and Selected Poems: 1975–2001.

who was buried in a cove of ocean.

Well, a key, technically. Waltz Key Basin, in Florida. The water there was shallow and calm, and it spit her bloated, waterlogged body back on shore four days after Roddie put her there. I was three years old at the time, so of course nobody told me any of this. All they told me was that I wouldn't be seeing my mom anymore because she was in heaven now. We weren't a religious family, so I had absolutely no idea what that meant. I still don't.

Ah, ah beats our lungs and we are racing into the waves.

There was no water in her lungs, according to the autopsy report I found when I was fourteen and got good at Google. Which means she was dead when she was dumped. She was drowned before she drowned, and I have spent many morbid hours since I read that report researching what exactly it feels like to be strangled to death. If Roddie compressed her carotid arteries, she would have blacked out and died quickly. But if he crushed her windpipe, it would have been long and tortuous and she would have been awake for all of it. Did you know that if your attacker is using his bare hands, as Roddie did, it can take you up to five whole minutes to die? Five minutes. At my old high school, five minutes of Mr. G's British lit class could feel like a thousand years. So even though I have tried, I can't imagine what five minutes of relentless pressure on your airway must feel like, your brain screaming for oxygen, and all the while as you kick and struggle and claw in a losing fight for your life, the face of your murderer— the man you thought you loved enough to run away with, abandoning your husband and your kid for—hangs over you. This is why, whenever teachers and counselors and therapists and whoever else try to lecture me about how bad choices have consequences, I always have to laugh. Who knows this better than I do? My mom made a bad choice when she chose to blow up her family and take off with some creep she met at a real estate conference. And, damn, did it ever have a consequence.

I snap shut Joy Harjo and consider Vera's theory of hereditary suffering, of how pain is passed down like a mutated gene from one generation to the next.

If it is true, then I am fucked.

14

"SO," VIVIAN SAYS. "You made it through your first week. How's it going so far?"

"Well, let's see." I'm sitting cross-legged on her big leather chair and picking at a piece of dried granola from breakfast that's stuck to my leggings. "I hate my dad and stepmom. I want some McDonald's and a cup of coffee. I want to look at Instagram. I want to look at a male human. Not even touch one, necessarily. Just *look* at one."

"On the bright side, I hear your classes are going well."

"They're independent study. It's not like they're hard. You just, like, sit in front of a computer and answer practice questions."

"If you get bored, maybe you could tutor some of the other girls. I hear you're something of an algebra whiz."

"I don't tutor. That's what teachers get paid for."

"Did you know that 'algebra' comes from an Arabic word?"

"No, I did not."

"*Al-jabr*. It means 'reunion of broken parts.'"

"Oh, I get it. You're going for profundity today. I, the

broken girl, find solace in a discipline that puts broken parts back together."

"I'm just telling you where the meaning of the word comes from. Etymology interests me. Are you always this defensive?"

"Pretty much."

"Well," she says, trying a different tack, "it looks like you've made a few friends. I've seen you hanging around with Vera and Trinity quite a bit. Madison, too."

"Yeah." I look out the window. It's been raining constantly, a cold, steady drizzle that, the girls tell me, should be turning into snow any day now. "Vera and Trinity are pretty cool. Madison is . . . tolerable."

"Tell me about your friends back home. What were they like?"

"I didn't have any friends back home."

"Really? None at all?"

"I mean, I had *people.* My phone was always blowing up. Dealers, fuckboys, moth girls, that kind of thing. But I didn't have actual *friends.* We were just people, usually available to each other to get into some shit. That was good enough for me."

"Was it?"

"Yep."

Vivian steeples her fingers and shoots me her therapist's signature tell-me-more look. I roll my eyes.

"It's not that I didn't *want* friends. But I also liked looking at people in terms of what we could do for each other. There was no messiness. No gray areas. No commitments. If that makes sense."

"It does, though I have to say, it sounds pretty clinical to me."

"Maybe, but at least we were being real with each other. I can't stand fakeness."

"You value honesty."

"Yeah. I do."

"Would you say that honesty is one of your core values?"

"If I were the type of person who used annoying therapy lingo, then yes, I would say that. Definitely."

"And yet you've lied to your parents so many times."

"Not my parents. My dad and stepmom."

She raises an eyebrow at that and writes something down on her legal pad.

"And anyway, you're wrong. I *used* to lie to Dad and Alanna all the time. But I stopped all that a few months ago."

"Why?"

"It was the day my dad took my bedroom door off its hinges to keep me from sneaking out. He thought he was being a badass, right? Really laying down the law. But it was so stupid! I was like, *That's what you think is going to be the thing that controls me?*"

"Was he trying to control you, do you think? Or was he trying to protect you?"

"Who cares? Every time I saw my stupid door leaning up

against the wall in the garage, I actually felt sorry for him. I realized my dad was just a person. Older than me, obviously, and with more money. But no more powerful. And there was nothing he or anybody else could really do to stop me from doing what I wanted."

"Until they sent you here."

"Yeah. Until they sent me here. But they didn't send me here because of all the lies I told them. They sent me here because I *stopped* lying to them."

"That's an interesting take. Tell me more."

"It's like you said last week. Our society hasn't figured out how to deal with difficult women. Especially difficult young women. My dad and Alanna were pissed, more than anything, that I shattered the illusion we had all agreed upon, that I do them the courtesy of putting in a marginal effort to pretend I'm not a fuckup and they do *me* the courtesy of marginally pretending to believe me. But when I stopped lying to them, they couldn't pretend anymore. So they sent me here instead—punching Alanna was just the excuse they'd been waiting for."

"That's a really interesting perspective, Mia."

"You know what I've noticed, Vivian?"

"What?"

"That when you tell me what I say is interesting, what you really mean is that I'm right."

15

IT'S TUESDAY AFTERNOON, and it still hasn't stopped raining. I've forgotten my notebook for history independent study, so Ms. Jean gives me a five-minute pass to go back to my dorm and get it. I run across the soaked, deserted quad, slide my key card in the front door, and duck into Birchwood just as a jag of lightning blazes across the sky. Mary Pat isn't big on downtime, and the dorm is totally deserted. Or at least that's what I think, until I walk into my bedroom and jump back, a scream gathering strength in the middle of my chest.

There, placed neatly in the middle of our writing desk, face turned toward the window as if contemplating the oak trees, is a decapitated head, crowned with silky yellow curls.

I collapse against the doorframe and try to do my breaths, but it's not working. I feel this howl pressing up through my body, working its way to my throat—

"*Mia!*"

A person, shaped like Madison but not Madison, shoots up from the top bunk.

"Stop! Mia! What's wrong?"

This not-Madison is talking with Madison's voice.

Since I can't speak, I just point with a single violently trembling finger to the dismembered head.

Not-Madison leaps down from the top bunk and flicks on the desk lamp.

"Who—"

"It's me," she says, coming toward me and flagrantly breaking the Rule of Six Inches by grabbing my hands. "I have really bad cramps and Swizzie was already asleep in the nurse's station because she has strep, so Nurse Melanie gave me permission to come lie down in our room before lunch. Hey. It's *me*."

I look at the face—it's Madison's face, wearing Madison's glasses, but her hair is wispy and mouse brown and missing in giant patches. The hairline starts at the crown of the head, the forehead a long arc, smooth as an egg.

"That's just my *wig*."

I look from her face to the pile of yellow curls on the desk. She reaches over and turns the dismembered head so that it's facing me, and now I see that the hair has been brushed carefully and arranged around a blank oval of Styrofoam.

"You're . . ." I look at her, pull my hands away. "You're bald?"

"I mean." She runs a hand shyly along her gaping forehead. "In places."

"Do you have *cancer*?"

"Ha! Maybe if I had cancer, people would actually have some *empathy*, instead of just thinking I'm a freak." She smiles a little sadly and walks over to pet the silky strands of her wig as if it's some sort of beloved pet. "Have you ever heard of trichotillomania?"

I shake my head.

"It's a BFRB. A body-focused repetitive behavior. Sort of like the nail biting, just even less socially acceptable. I pull out my hair when I'm stressed."

"Madison." I know I'm gawking at her, but I can't help it. Without her blond curls, she looks so defenseless, so *damaged*. "You must be *really* stressed."

"Oh, this is nothing! This is *way* better than it was when I first got here. At least I've learned to leave my eyebrows alone. And my bottom lashes. The top ones, those are trickier. Those are just so *satisfying* to pull, you know? I have this whole ritual of pulling them out and then, like, lining them up on my wrist and seeing how long they can stay there without falling off. Does that sound weird?"

"Please don't make me answer that question."

"Well, trichotillomania is a lot more common than you'd think, judgy-pants. And anyway, I'm improving. My parents and Mary Pat and Carolyn have an agreement: once it *all* starts to grow back in, every last strand, then I can come home. Mary Pat thinks as long as I don't regress, I'll be out of here by the spring. In time for junior prom, if I can find anyone pathetic enough to take me!"

Before I can stop myself, I reach out and run a hand across her head. In the places where she's torn out her hair, the skin is delicate and soft, like a newborn's. It's hard to believe there was ever hair growth there at all.

"Holy *shit*, Madison."

"Don't! Six inches!" She ducks away from my hand, her face twisted up in a pout. "How come you don't judge Trinity? She wore acrylic nails from fifth grade straight through to when Nurse Melanie soaked them off at intake! And aren't those just wigs for your fingers? Nobody thinks *she's* a freak."

"Oh, relax." I sit heavily on my bed. "I don't think you're a freak. You just scared me, that's all—I thought someone killed you."

She pauses. "You thought I was dead?"

"Yes! It's dark in here, this school is full of lunatics with pasts shrouded in secrecy, and your fucking stunt double of a head is just sitting there on our writing desk!"

"Wow." She sits down next to me. "You were really upset, huh?"

"Well, *yeah*."

"You *like* me." A smile twitches on her face.

"If your standard of liking someone is *not* wanting them to be violently murdered and dismembered then yeah, Madison, I guess I like you."

"Well, I like you, too, Mia." Her smile widens into such a wedge of earnestness that I have to look away. She reaches over to hug me, and I try to bat her arm away, but she is *here* for this hug, so she feints past and wraps her arms around me anyway.

I will admit this to no one: it feels pretty nice.

16

TRINITY HAS THIS giant bin of nail stuff, and on the Friday of my second week, during constructive relaxation, Vera borrows it and invites me down to her room to give ourselves pedicures under the surly supervision of Dee, who is straddled at Vera's desk chair, scrolling through her phone and loudly eating an apple. I still have some chipped red paint on my toes left over from the summer, but when I dig through the bin, I can't find any nail polish remover.

"Banned substance," Dee barks, looking up briefly from her screen to glare at me. "Didn't you read your handbook?"

"That's dumb. How am I supposed to take this red off my toes?"

"Nail polish remover contains alcohol,"[15] Vera says as she shakes up a bottle of jet black organic polish. "Girls might try to drink it."

"What kind of psycho would drink *nail* polish remover?"

---

[15] Red Oak Academy student handbook section 8.5: personal grooming—cosmetics: banned personal grooming items include but are not limited to: perfume, aerosol hair sprays and deodorants, liquid eyeliner, depilatories, baby oil, straight and disposable razors, nail scissors, tweezers, Q-tips, whitening toothpaste, hydrogen peroxide, mirrored makeup compacts, and mouthwash.

"I've had it a couple times," says Soleil. Vera's roommate is a shifty-eyed blond junkie from Los Angeles who makes her own clothes—or used to, before she came here and lost access to needles, both the sewing kind and the vein-injecting kind. When you ask her a question, it takes her so long to respond that when I first met her I thought she'd somehow smuggled in some edibles or something.

"Are you serious? You drank *nail polish remover?*"

"Mm-hm."

"What did it taste like?"

Soleil fixes her limp stare on me for so long I'm about to repeat myself. Finally she says, "Worse than mouthwash, better than pruno."[16]

Dee makes a little grunt of disgust and turns her attention back to her phone while Vera bursts out laughing. "Oh my God, Soleil. They can say what they want about me, but for my money, you're hands down the wildest bitch at Red Oak."

Soleil's face breaks out into a slow grin. On my first night, Madison pointed Soleil out to me as she brushed her teeth dreamily at the communal bathroom sinks and told me that her dad was some sort of big-time music producer, the kind whose name you don't recognize but who owns half the beats on Top 40. She grew up in a glass palace in the Hollywood

---

[16] Also known as prison wine, pruno is a homemade alcoholic beverage made with ketchup packets and fermented rotten fruit. Apparently girls used to make it here by smuggling the ingredients out of the cafeteria and brewing it under their beds. This is why our pockets have to be sewn shut, and also why, if you're the kind of person who enjoys condiments, so long as you're living in Red Oak you better learn to like your fries dipped in mayo.

Hills, complete with an infinity pool that fed directly into the Pacific Ocean, and before she came here she attended that famous school all the Kardashians went to. With her heroin-chic good looks and her trust fund/burnout vibe, it occurs to me that Soleil and Xander would probably make a great couple. I wonder how much she knows about rare French Bordeaux.

"See, Mia," Vera says, furrowing her brow with concentration as she brushes the glossy black paint across her toenails, "Soleil and I have this East Coast–West Coast rivalry thing going. She's Tupac, I'm Biggie."

"Don't make that comparison, baby," Soleil drawls from her perch on her bed, legs in the lotus position. "We're white, and that's culturally appropriative."

"First of all," Vera says, moving onto her other foot, "*you're* white. *I'm* Arab."

"Half."

"Still. Not the same. Second of all, *you're a white person with dreadlocks*, so you don't get to yell at people for being culturally appropriative."

Soleil sniffs, uncrosses her legs, and reclines back on her bottom bunk with her hands folded behind her head.

"And third," Vera continues, "we *are* like Pac and Biggie, not racially, not culturally, but simply due to the fact that I'm pretty positive neither one of us will make it out of our twenties alive."

"Vera!" I look up from my toenails, which I've painted red to match the chipped layer beneath. "Way to be morbid."

"Seriously," agrees Dee.

"What? It's true!"

Soleil looks up at me with her big blue California eyes and nods sadly in agreement.

"Look," Vera says. "I know Mary Pat goes out of her way to try and differentiate Red Oak from, like, prisons or drug rehab facilities, but the fact is, we have about the same recidivism rates as those places. Isn't that right, Dee?"

"Leave me out of it." Dee picks at a curl of apple skin stuck between her teeth. "I'm just the muscle."

"Well, it *is* true, okay? When they get out of here, the vast majority of girls fall right back into the crazy shit that got them *in* here. It might take a week, it might take a year—but the odds are against us. Just look at the three girls who came to Red Oak the same month I did. They all matured[17] last year. And today? Jackie's a stripper, Olivia's a junkie, and poor Makayla's dead."

"Stop gossiping," Dee yawns. "I could write you up for this."

This elicits a brief moment of silence from all three of us. I concentrate on finishing my nails. I want to ask how Makayla died, but I don't want to get written up and I'm also not sure I really want to know.

---

[17] Maturation is the final step in a Red Oak girl's journey. Staying true to the metaphorical growth cycles of the red oak tree, it is the term the school uses in place of "graduation."

"Now, when *I* get out," Soleil finally says, "I don't *want* to roll with the same old crowd, get back into hard drugs and all that . . . and I'm gonna try not to. I swear I am. But it still might happen. And if it does, that will *suck*. Because I really *don't* want to die." She shrugs, stifles a yawn. "I probably will, though. What can you do?"

"Yeah," Vera says quietly. "What can you do?"

"Um," says Dee, looking incredulously between them. "A *lot?*"

We all burst out laughing at that, because one of the things about the outside world that you miss in a place like this is the chance to shock people. But later, as I walk back to my room on my heels so my pedicure doesn't smear, I find that our laughter wasn't enough to dislodge the dark feeling that began welling up inside of me when Vera first bought up the question of dying young.

17

WHEN I WAS IN EIGHTH GRADE, my homeroom teacher, a harried but well-meaning geriatric named Mrs. Jones, recruited me to join the math scholars club. This involved weekly meetings, word-problem-athons (don't ask), and matching T-shirts,[18] culminating in a research project that we had to present to a citywide competition.

I did my project on the Twenty-Seven Club—the group of famous musicians who all died suddenly and tragically at the age of twenty-seven. My goal was to find out whether there was a real statistical significance to the number of famous people who died at that age, but my findings determined that only 1 percent of rock-star deaths since the 1950s occurred to twenty-seven-year-old people. In other words, the whole idea of twenty-seven being a cursed, mystical year of death was more of a cultural myth than a mathematical reality. Which, anticlimactic as that was, didn't stop me from winning first place and a thousand-dollar college scholarship voucher. *What an interesting topic!* One of the panel judges

---

[18] Slogan across chest: WHERE IT'S HIP TO B^2.

had said as she pinned a ribbon to the heinous floral blouse Alanna had purchased for me for the occasion. *What made you choose it?*

Well, some of the coolest people of all time died at that age, I answered in a tremulous voice. *Kurt Cobain. Jimi Hendrix. Kristen Pfaff. Janis Joplin. Amy Winehouse.*

My mother.[19]

Tonight, I'm thinking about the Twenty-Seven Club.

I'm thinking about how ever since I got to Red Oak, I've reassured myself again and again that I'm not like these other girls. I'm normal bad, you see, and they're *bad* bad. *Crazy* bad. *Mentally unstable* bad. But after my conversation with Vera and Soleil tonight, it occurs to me that maybe I'm not as different from these girls as I first thought.

Because I, too, have always held a secret belief that I'm fated to die suddenly, tragically, and way too young.

I think about how my life these past few years has been a kind of dance around this belief, how so many of my actions have been a dare to see if it's really true. If I was back home right now, take any given weekend and I'd probably be squeezing myself into something tight and short, getting ready to head out for the night—school night or not. I'd have my Juul charged up, my hair curled around my shoulders in

---

[19] I didn't say this last one out loud, though, of course. First, because my mother was a real estate agent and not a rock star, and second, I wanted to win because I was the best, not because the committee felt sorry for me.

long waves, my fake ID and cash I'd stolen from Alanna's wallet nestled into the pockets of my cropped faux-leather moto jacket.[20] Do I miss those kinds of nights? Not really, to be honest. What I miss is the beginning ritual, blasting music in my bedroom—Kesha or Cardi, Nicki or Ari, Gaga or King Woman, my dad's old Guns N' Roses and Zeppelin albums, or my mom's Hole and Bikini Kill CDs from when she was my age. I miss sitting on the edge of my bed as the beats pulsed around me, pulling black nylons up my freshly shaven legs, the way my stockinged feet slipped so cool and smooth into my boots. I miss the blending of the shadow, the smudging of the liner, the gentle squeeze of the lash curler, the minty tingle of plumping gloss as it slicked over my lips. I miss that first step out the door, the quiet unfurling inside of me, the giving of myself to the game of chance that was the night.

There is great power in this, the ability to telegraph to the world how much you just don't give a shit. Boys find it sexy. Girls, too.

But here's the truth: I *did* give a shit.

Those jolts of panic that would rock through me whenever I realized I could never call back the control I had relinquished told me so. The moments when excitement curdled into fear, when things no longer felt like a game. Like the night last summer when me and Eve met some boys

---

[20] Also stolen.

down by the Montrose Beach boathouse. One of them had a pickup truck, and we hopped in the bed and went for a ride. Everything was so much fun until the boy who was driving—whose name I've since forgotten—decided to pull onto Lake Shore Drive. Soon we were speeding along the water so fast that I had to close my eyes to keep them from drying up, the lake wind slashing at my face, but he kept going faster and faster, and me and Eve couldn't do anything but cling to the sides of the truck bed and scream, knowing that with one quick swerve or sudden brake we'd be thrown over the side to explode against the asphalt, girl-shaped missiles in the night.

Later, when I got home, I couldn't stop shaking and I couldn't sleep. I listened to Amy and Janis and Aaliyah,[21] but I found that any romantic notion I may have had about dying young had blown away on the Lake Shore Drive wind.

It scared me—just not enough to change me.

Later that same summer I almost died again. Me and some kids from school snuck up to the roof of a carpet warehouse in Goose Island to smoke weed and watch the Navy Pier fireworks. Me and this boy Adrian were sitting together on a skylight, passing a joint back and forth, when the glass cracked beneath us. We jumped up just in time, a second before the whole thing gave way, crashing down into a million pieces to the concrete thirty or forty feet below.

---

[21] Not, technically, a member of the Twenty-Seven Club, since she was only twenty-two when she died in a plane crash.

Lying here now, under my thin, itchy blanket, with the mute trees swaying outside, I shiver, remembering. Why didn't I die that night? Or so many other nights, when my luck could have—*should* have—swung in the other direction? It's just another reason, as if I needed one, not to believe in God. Because if God were real, why would they cut down so many kind and decent people in the prime of their lives, so many brilliant artists, and then decide to spare a piece of shit like me?

18

FOR HALLOWEEN, I get a homemade card in the mail from Lauren and Lola. On the cover of the folded construction paper is a drawing of a ghost, the typical white-sheet-looking one, except it's topped with curly black hair, bleached lavender at the tips, and purple eye shadow smudged around its circular black eyes—so I guess it's supposed to be the ghost of me—or at least, the me I was before I came here and they chopped off my colored ends and stopped letting me wear most of my makeup.

MIA!!! It says in shakily printed block letters on the inside of the card.

WE MISS U!!!

WE LOVE U!!!

U ARE BOO-TIFUL!!!

I miss the twins, too. I love them, too. I, too, think they are boo-tiful.

Always have.

I remember the summer they were born, the summer I turned eleven. They arrived six weeks early, so tiny that they had to spend a week in the hospital before we could bring them home. When they got here, they mostly slept, but when they were awake they cried and cried, these little mewling wails that filled the whole house, and they'd kick their tiny wrinkled legs and ball their fists so that all I wanted to do was pick them up and rock them until they slept against me, two tiny loaves of warmth against my chest.

Not that Alanna ever let me hold them much. Or feed them, either. She'd read on some online parenting blog that if she fed the babies formula from a bottle, they would grow up to be stupid, so she breastfed them constantly, even if it meant she got, like, one hour of sleep per night. She cried even more than the twins did, and she could go days without showering or brushing her hair. That summer, whenever I came home from soccer camp, she'd be sitting in the family room, lights off, blinds pulled, air-conditioning blasting, topless and wearing the same stained pair of yoga pants, holding a baby to each boob and staring at *Judge Mathis* without actually watching it.

"What's wrong with her?" I asked Dad one night when he took me out for ice cream so I wouldn't feel neglected.

"Having a baby, let alone two . . . it's a hard adjustment," he said.

"Was Mom like this? When you guys brought me home?"

"You were a pretty easy baby," he answered, digging into his mint chocolate chip. "And there was only one of you. But yeah, she had a hard time, too."

"She did? Like how?"

"Just normal stuff. Sleeplessness. Hormones. You know."

But I didn't.

"The thing with your mother," he finally said, poking at his ice cream as he very pointedly refused to look at my face, "was that she loved being *your* mom. But she didn't necessarily love being *a* mom, if that makes sense."

"I mean." I stared at him. I knew that if I stared hard enough, he'd eventually have to look at me, and soon enough, he did. "Not really."

He sighed and put down his spoon. "Your mom, Mia. She was a complicated woman. A wonderful, complicated woman. She had a difficult history and had many different issues and she thought—we both did—that maybe having a baby could fix . . ." He made his this-conversation-is-giving-me-a-headache face and trailed off. I was about to ask him what it was that I had failed to fix for her, and whether that was the reason she left us. But he changed the subject quickly.

"Could you do me a favor, honey? When you're around during the afternoons, after camp, could you help Alanna out with the twins?"

"But, like, how? She won't even let me hold them."

"So help her in other ways. Laundry. Dishwasher. Vacuum. That kind of thing." He pointed his spoon at me and smiled. "You know what to do, right? You took care of me all those years before I met her, didn't you?"

Which wasn't true, of course, because little kids, even gifted little kids, aren't exactly up to the task of running a household. My grandma had done the bulk of that, before she'd died. But what he said *felt* true—it reminded me that our history went deeper than his and Alanna's, that we were still a unit, that we would always be allies no matter how many new babies he and Alanna decided to have together.

So I tried.

One morning, after the twins had been up all night, I came home from camp to find Alanna passed out on the couch with the girls sleeping in the portable bassinet next to her. Even though I'd tried to come in quietly, Lauren woke up and started bawling. I was afraid her cries would shatter this rare moment of peace, and the house was already spotless, so I decided I'd take her for a walk. I strapped the carrier over my shoulders, the way I'd seen Alanna do it, and clicked Lauren inside. As soon as we started moving, she fell immediately into a contented sleep, her little forehead resting against the fabric of my tank top. I walked all over the neighborhood with her, waving at people I knew, so proud to be caring for her, my baby sister. *See?* I wanted to say to Alanna. *You were so afraid to trust me. Turns out, I'm a natural.*

I was only gone for an hour, but when I got back, Alanna was waiting for me, pacing on the front steps with her phone clutched in her hand.

"Where were you?" she demanded, her voice choked

because she was trying so hard to keep herself from screaming at me.

"I just took her for a walk," I said. "She was awake and I wanted to let you sleep."

"She's not a doll, Mia. You can't just take a brand-new baby somewhere without telling anyone. Without telling her *mother.*"

"Sorry." I swallowed hard, unsnapped the straps of the carrier, and handed Lauren over. "I was just trying to help."

"I know you were," Alanna said, softening now that she had proof I hadn't accidentally lost her baby or whatever. "It's just—*ask* me next time, okay?"

I pushed past her and went into the house. "Okay."

"Wait." Something about her voice pinned me in place and I turned around. "Did you put a hat on her?"

A hat. I had remembered almost everything. Almost.

"Please tell me you put a hat on her."

"We were only—"

"She's too little for sunscreen." Alanna began to pace the front stoop again. "They can't wear sunscreen until they're six months old at least. But still, if you didn't put a hat on her, you must have put sunscreen on her. Because if you didn't . . ."

I felt the tears springing to my eyes. I was so stupid. I was so unbelievably worthless and stupid. Lauren's little head, so thin-skinned and delicate, practically bald except for a few wisps of blond hair, was already darkening into an angry pink.

"Oh my God. You—go upstairs."

With the world's worst possible timing, Lauren chose that exact moment to wake up and begin wailing.

"Go upstairs!"

I did as I was told—headed toward the landing, and when I turned back once, I saw Alanna clutching Lauren against her chest, examining the damage I'd done with a look of wild, furious all-consuming love. She had never, of course, looked at me that way, not even when I'd gotten hit in the face during a sixth-grade softball game and broken my nose. It was a mother's look, filled with a mother's love, and it could never be replicated or replaced.

My dad came home from work that night and found me lying under the covers in my canopy bed. I thought he was going to yell at me, but instead he kicked off his oxfords and climbed in next to me. He put his arms around me, rested his stubbly chin on my shoulder, and just held me for a long time, as if I were still a baby, too. Which made me feel so much better and also so much worse. My dad—no, everybody in my family—deserved so much better than what I was. Even my mom knew this. It was probably why she left.

I look down now at the Halloween card in front of me. *You are BOO-tiful!!!* All the exclamation marks have little pumpkins instead of dots. I hold the card against my heart until my ache for them passes, as sharp and cresting as a period cramp.

19

RED OAK ACADEMY
STUDENT SCHEDULE
DEMPSEY, MIA
ID #47813

6:30—*first bell*

7:00—*breakfast / kitchen cleanup / food prep*

8:00—*group chat*

8:30–9:30—*English/language arts*

9:35–10:45—*foreign language independent study*

10:50–11:50—*mathematics independent study*

12:00–12:40—*lunch / kitchen cleanup*

12:45–1:45—*individual therapy (M/W)*

Dorm chores (Tu/Th)

Bathroom chores (F)

1:50–2:50—*nature connection/physical education*

2:55–3:55—*social studies independent study*

4:00–4:45—*constructive relaxation*

5:00–5:55—*dinner / kitchen cleanup / food prep*

6:00–7:00—homework
7:05–8:00—constructive relaxation
8:05–8:30—personal hygiene
8:35–9:00—lights dimmed
9:00—lights out

Day after day, each minute of my life is parceled out, measured by somebody else's clock, then boxed away forever. Minutes and hours and days of *my* life that I'll never get back—and it's worse than prison because I don't even have a release date to hang my hopes on. I look forward, each night, to lights-out, because the only time I'm free is when I'm sleeping.

20

RED OAK RULES DICTATE that you're not allowed to speak to your family back home for the first two weeks of your imprisonment. Mary Pat says this is a way to speed up the process of acclimating to life here, to help "reroute your neuron loops to your new reality." Vera says it's to prevent you from begging your parents to bring you home right when they're at their most vulnerable and most likely to say yes.

Guess which explanation I believe?

On the Sunday afternoon that marks the beginning of my third week at Red Oak, Dee escorts me to the admin office for my first session of family therapy. Mary Pat and Vivian are waiting for me in the demonic Cracker Barrel office, standing next to Mary Pat's big desktop monitor. My dad and Alanna are already on-screen, waiting for me on the family room couch, pressed close together and clasping hands like they're bracing themselves for a troubled teen tornado.

"Where are the twins?" I ask before I sit down.

"Unforunately, Mia," Mary Pat says, patiently indicating a chair in front of the camera, "conversations with siblings are a privilege that can only be earned in your second month, with good behavior."

I sit down with a sigh.

"Oh, Mia." Alanna gasps as soon as I come into view. "You look so—so well-*rested*." I can see that the two black eyes I gave her have faded into a topography of yellowing bruises. Couldn't she have thrown on some concealer for this meeting? She probably wants to make me look as bad as possible to Mary Pat and Vivian, to convince them I'm super-extra troubled, and to keep me here, and out of their lives, for as long as she can.

"Hi, baby," Dad says. His voice is tired, and his eyes are glassy, like he's stoned or something, but since I know he's never touched a drug in his life I can only assume that he's been crying. Which makes me feel like a massive pile of shit.

Sorry, I say in my head. *If it makes you feel any better, I hate me, too.*

"Hey," I say.

"So, um. How's it going up there?"

"Well, let's see." I begin counting off on my fingers. "You guys had me kidnapped. They took my phone. They made me take my clothes off so they could body-cavity-search me. I can't use nail polish remover because it has alcohol in it and they're afraid I might try to drink it. Oh! And my roommate is a domestic terrorist who eats her own skin."

"Mia," Dad says, cracking his knuckles. "Don't act like

this came out of nowhere. You've been on a downward trajectory for a long time now. You've—it's become impossible for us to go it alone with you anymore."

"Oh, I know," I say, smiling cruelly. "I've read the literature. *Parenting is never easy. But it should never be this hard. And if it is, just get rid of your kid!*"

"See?" Alanna cries, looking to Mary Pat for backup. "See the anger? The cutting comments? The, just, *relentless* snarkiness?"

"Of course I'm angry!" I shout. "I know I shouldn't have hit you, okay? I know that was wrong, and I'm sorry or whatever. But it doesn't mean I belong *here*, surrounded by cutters and internet porn stars and suicide cases and *fire starters!*"

"Fire starters?" Dad, alarmed, looks over at Mary Pat and runs a hand through his already-thinning hair. "Jeez."

"We have, in the past, treated girls with fire-setting issues," Mary Pat replies calmly. "There are none currently enrolled at Red Oak, though. And even if there were, Mia would not be in danger. If we don't allow our girls to have nail polish remover, do you really believe we'd allow them access to matches?"

"Mia," Alanna whines, her eyes filling with tears—she is a *classic* example of someone who uses crying as a tool of manipulation—"I know it's hard for you to understand this, but we feel that you *do* belong at Red Oak. We love you so much, but it's like, all the love we give you, you just suck it up and spit it right back into our faces."

"*You* love me?" I can't help myself. I start laughing.

Alanna's mouth hangs open for an instant. "Of *course* I love you, Mia. How could you even—"

"Do you know what she said to me that day?" I ask Dad. "Before I punched her?"

Dad clears his throat, glances at his wife, then employs his superhero skill: answering a question without actually answering it.

"We had a conversation," he says. "There are no secrets between Alanna and me. You didn't leave us much of a choice, Mia. We just felt very strongly that you needed a *complete* separation from your current life, from this Xander character, and even from your sisters, from *us*—"

I can't stand to hear them talk anymore, to hear Xander's name in my dad's mouth, to hear Xander's name at all, as if *he's* the problem, as if he even fucking matters. I can't stand to look at their faces, both guilty and accusatory, and I can't stand to see our kitchen through the doorway behind the couch, can't stand to remember the freedom of throwing open the fridge whenever I wanted, of digging out some leftover pizza and eating it in front of my laptop. Of going where I wanted and doing what I wanted. Of being a normal teenager: a little wild maybe, and definitely making lots of mistakes, but figuring life out. Instead of now, where I'm locked up in a place where all temptation is taken away and

I'm not even given the *choice* to do the right thing anymore. I'm sure all the kids at school are talking even more shit about me than they did when I was still around. Or maybe not. Maybe they've all forgotten I exist. I can't decide which is worse. The thoughts press in, faster and faster, pushing the tears into my eyes, and since I am *not* a manipulative crier, since I am a person who believes that crying is weak and self-indulgent and useless, since I refuse to let Alanna know she has the power to *make* me cry, I get to my feet and jab the end call button.

"Mia, wait!" calls Vivian, but when I run out of Mary Pat's office, slamming the door behind me, she has the good sense not to follow me.

21

WHAT ALANNA SAID TO ME
RIGHT BEFORE I HIT HER

You know what you are to these boys, right?
Nothing but a punch line to laugh about with his buddies.
And in the moment,
nothing
but
a
warm
hole.

22

I STILL HAVE SOME TIME to kill before I have to show up for dinner, so I decide to go for a walk. The air is sharp and flinty, but I can't head back to my room for my coat because that would require speaking to the girls in Birchwood and right now I don't feel like speaking to anyone. I pull the sleeves of my sweatshirt over my fists, set my shoulders, and walk toward the trail behind the library, the one that leads into the woods and down to Lake Onamia. The sun is just beginning to set, because here at Red Oak we eat dinner at five, like old people.

Campus is quiet enough to begin with, especially when you're a city kid like me and aren't used to it. But once you step into the woods, it's even creepier. It's like all those pine and oak trees absorb any stray sound, and the silence becomes absolute. That's why I almost never go for walks, even though the walking trails, peppered as they are with security cameras, are one of the few freedoms we're allowed, given the Red Oak belief in the HEALING PROPERTIES OF MOTHER NATURE™. As the silence envelops me now, I think about turning back, but the air is fresh against my skin, and my limbs feel strong and twitchy. I feel like a penned-in horse, aching for movement. Two weeks at Red Oak. The longest I've gone since I was fourteen without smoking or drinking or pills. Physically, I feel very good and clean and strong. Emotionally, it's more complicated.

By the time I reach the marshy edge of Lake Onamia, waving with cattails and duckweed and droning with the low buzz of insects, the sun is gone and the sky is a globe over the water. The stars are bright points of light glittering everywhere, and beyond them swirls a white veil of the more distant stars. The longer I look up, the more I can see. I sit on a damp log—perhaps even the famous log of the Red Oak Academy brochures—and watch as the whole sky becomes a lacy pattern of inlaid pricks of fire. I wonder, does the sky always look this magnificent and I've just never noticed? I wonder why it is that the most beautiful things are always the easiest to miss. I wonder how it is that I could go from being a real person, a whole person, a person with a soul and dreams, to being nothing but a punch line and a warm hole.

I guess it started halfway through my first year of high school, when my honors integrated science class took a field trip to the planetarium. I was the only freshman in the class; I'd been placed there because of my test scores. No one really talked to me, not even my lab partner, Scottie Curry. Scottie was on the Academic Bowl team, with big ears and even bigger glasses, but there was something sexy about him. For starters, he was older than me—a senior!—and whenever we did a lab he would push up the sleeves of his hipster-dork sweater to reveal thick, hairy man wrists. He was totally indifferent, or maybe just unaware, of his objective lack of popularity, because he walked around school with the same kind of swagger you might see on a star football player. Which I liked. But what I liked even more was the way he recognized right away that even though I was an underclassman and also sort of a deadbeat, with my black clothes and ever-present earbuds, I still was smarter than he was. It's not like he was friendly, exactly, but whenever we got different results on our labs, he always deferred to me, and we got straight A's on everything we turned in. We were an unlikely team, and I crushed on him, hugely and secretly, without daring to think he'd ever like me back. It was a nice distraction, fantasizing about him, especially because this was right around the time I found my mom's autopsy report on the internet. Sometimes I thought he was flirting with me, but I figured it was probably all in my head—this was a senior, a guy who had applied early admission to Princeton and had a decent chance of actually being accepted. But then, right before our first semester exam, he asked me to come over to his house to study. I told my friend Marnie about it, and she said, "He totally wants to bang you," and I rolled my eyes and laughed it off, but secretly I was excited—a boy had never wanted me before, as far as I knew. Before I went over there, I shaved my legs and took some extra time with my hair, painted on some lip stain and flicked mascara across my lashes. I put on my tightest jeans and my lowest-cut top and slicked shimmery jasmine-scented body lotion across what little cleavage I had.

I got over there, and when he opened the door he sort of stared at me. "You look different," he said, and I said, "Thanks," and then immediately felt stupid because I didn't know whether he was complimenting me. No one was home at his house, and I thought we were going to study in his kitchen, maybe his basement, but instead he led me upstairs to his bedroom. I'd never been in a boy's room before. It smelled like body spray and feet. We sat on his bed and took out our science stuff and studied for a little bit, but I couldn't concentrate, and he couldn't seem to, either. He kept shifting around and looking uncomfortable. I wondered if he was trying to cover up a boner or something. Erections were situations of the male body that, at the time, I only knew about conceptually and which I sort of considered too absurd to be a real thing. And maybe it was for that reason that I was struck by a bolt of impulsive courage, or maybe it was just a desire not to leave Scottie's house without a story for Marnie, who had already texted me about twenty times, looking for updates. Whatever the case, I went for it: I leaned across my lab notebook and I kissed him.

I kissed *him*.

Whenever I think about this day—which is not often, because what's the point of picking at an old crusty wound?—I always remind myself of this. It went so wrong so quickly, but *I* was the one who put it all in motion. Which I feel like is probably a good metaphor for my life in general.

Anyway. So, yeah, I kissed him. His eyes opened wide at first, and I stared into them, brown hurricanes behind fingerprint-smudged glass frames, and then they fluttered closed and I knew I didn't have to feel stupid anymore—I had made the right decision. I was worried I wouldn't know how to kiss, but what I realized was that everybody's born knowing how to kiss, just like everybody's born knowing how to breathe, how to cry. We kissed for a while over our notebooks, and that was nice, really nice, but then everything started to move very fast. The best part of the whole experience, when I think about it now, was the last second before he pushed himself into me, when I looked up at him, my hair loose around my shoulders. At that moment, I sort of felt like an actress in my own life. But, like, a *good* actress. In a good movie. What I mean is, I felt like a real grown-up. A real *woman*. But then, as Scottie began to lower himself on top of me, the feeling passed. I understood that I wasn't an actress and this wasn't a movie and I wasn't a woman, at least not yet, and I wasn't ready to do this, at least not yet. But Scottie had already taken his glasses off and was looking at my body with something that I recognized as desire but thought might definitely also be love. How was I expected to know the difference? How was I expected to know anything about boys or relationships or sex or love? Isn't that the kind of thing you're supposed to learn about from your mother? And besides, I was a *freshman*. I'd been to a million sessions with school counselors, talking about consent, about how no means no and yes means yes and the yes must be an *enthusiastic* yes, and that all felt so obvious, sitting at my school desk and looking at an awkward PowerPoint being delivered by an equally awkward teacher in a festive scarf and sensible shoes, but now that I was in it, *living* it, tangled in a boy's actual bed with a boy's actual hands on my actual body, none of that mattered. When I tried to find the words—"*No.*" "*Wait.*" "*Stop.*"—they wouldn't come.

"Um," I tried. But he wasn't listening. My body felt frozen, like a dead moth pinned inside a display case. I turned my face away and squeezed my eyes shut and went quiet and still as he fumbled with the condom he'd dug out of his nightstand. I felt like, if my body went quiet enough, that would be the screaming no that my mouth couldn't find the courage to say. I kept my eyes closed against the building pressure of tears and stayed very still as he lowered down and pressed inside of me, and it hurt, but I could stand it, and then nearly as soon as it had started he was trembling, then mumbling an apology, and that's how I knew it was over.

When I got home that night, I was *sure* that my dad would take one look at me and know what I'd done. He was my dad, and not just a regular dad but a widower dad who had raised me on his own for six whole years before he met Alanna. We had once been as close as two people could be. And even though that had faded a little, he still knew my moods, my behaviors, my soul, better than anyone on the planet. I prepared for this reality on the walk home from Scottie's house through the holiday-lit streets. I decided there was no point in lying or even obfuscating. When he looked at me and asked what had happened, I would simply tell him everything. It would be embarrassing, obviously, and he would not be happy, but I would tell him anyway because I knew he was the only person who could help me make sense of it, what it meant, who I was now. Maybe he would even tell me that it didn't mean anything at all. How could it, when the whole experience from the moment Scottie and I started kissing to the moment he wrapped the used condom in a Kleenex and tossed it onto the floor next to his bed, had lasted no more than ten minutes?

But when I got home, it turned out that the twins, who were toddlers at the time, had picked up some nasty bug at their daycare and were both engaged in *Exorcist* levels of vomiting. Alanna was bathing them while yelling frantically into the phone at urgent care while my dad was busy stripping their beds and stuffing everything down the laundry chute. He gave me a quick kiss on the top of my head as I stood in the middle of the front hall, watching this hive of activity, of parents caring for small, sick children, and suddenly my problems felt meaningless and my life felt small and silly. I went upstairs, crawled into bed, and slept for twelve hours. When I woke up in the morning the twins were still sick and my dad was still distracted. He never noticed a thing.

I thought I could try to put it behind me, maybe somehow work up the courage to ask Mr. Henderson for a new lab partner second semester and just pretend like nothing had ever happened. But that was not to be, because as it turned out, Scottie Curry had a girlfriend.

And apparently she somehow found out what we'd done.

A theater nerd, she was the head of the tech crew on the fall play. Not exactly Mean Girl material. But she had friends in our integrated science class, and they more than made up for it.

They were the ones, when we were on the bus riding to the planetarium the day we returned from semester break, who cough-shouted "Whore!" when I walked past them on the bus. Who twisted in their seats to pelt me with tampons and Cheez-Its and fruit snacks.

To Scottie they said nothing. Scottie and his girlfriend had worked it out. He had apologized or bought her flowers or told her I had seduced him and maybe I even had? I'd kissed him first. *I'd kissed him first.*

Whatever the case, Scottie and his girlfriend were cool.

With me, though, it was different.

These girls may have been seniors, but they weren't necessarily at the top of the pecking order of the social hierarchy. But I was lower, by a long shot. I was a freshman, not unpopular but worse than unpopular, because I didn't play sports or do clubs and I was also sort of trashy, a nobody with a murdered mom who dyed my hair weird colors and hung out with budding criminals like Marnie. What was I even *doing* in their honors class, let alone having sex with one of *their* guys, one of *their* friends' boyfriends? They took it very personally. That day, their heckling was like a dull throb, and they kept it up through most of the guided tour, grew bolder in the model space shuttle after Mr. Henderson announced we were free to explore on our own as long as we met up at the school bus entrance at one thirty.

"Slut."

"Pig."

"Cum dumpster."

"White trash."

At first I ignored them. In the model space shuttle, while they machine-gunned me with their words, I just stared up at the sleeping bags anchored to the wall and figured it could be worse: I could be an astronaut, forced to sleep standing up strapped to the wall every night for months and years as I hurtled at unimaginable speeds through the hostile cosmos.

I thought I could just continue ignoring them, but they kept getting closer to me. A few times they stepped on my heel and I had to lean down to pull my shoe back on. I started to panic—they were actually going to kick my ass, weren't they?—and then I ran. I literally ran away from them— which, of course, was the absolute worst thing I could do, because it showed my weakness and my fear. As soon as I took off they started to chase me, laughing, screaming their insults more loudly so other kids were laughing, too, bolder and bolder, and the hallways of the space shuttle got narrower and darker, and then I turned a corner and came upon a heavy rubber curtain, the kind you see in car washes, and I pushed it aside and ducked through.

And somehow, miraculously, I was free of them.

I had walked straight into outer space.

It was pitch-black, darker than anything I'd ever experienced in my life. The darkness had texture and weight, and all around me were the sounds of ambient whooshing and faraway explosions—the sounds of contracting stars, or of the womb. I had stepped into the quiet distant edge of the universe, or maybe into the past, back into my mother's body, but either way I was alone, alone. Scottie did not exist, and neither did those girls, or anyone or anything anchored to this world. I thought that if I called for my mother, she would hear me. I felt sure of it. I said her name into the darkness.

Mommy, I crooned, the word rusty on my lips, it having been eleven years since I'd uttered it. *Mommy. Help me.*

That's when I walked into a carpeted wall, and it thunked me right back into real life. I dug my phone from my pocket and fumbled for the flashlight app. Saw that I had not, after all, stepped through a rip in the dimensional fabric but only into a very well-constructed space-simulation booth—a part of the exhibit, just like the vertical sleeping bags.

But the weird thing was, I wasn't disappointed. Because fake or not, when I took a deep breath and stepped back through the curtain into real life, something had shifted inside of me. My scattered rage had gathered like the darkness, had coagulated into something I could now grab a hold of. Maybe my mother—strangled, discarded, unavenged—had heard me after all.

I knew that from now on, if somebody tried to fuck with me, I would never run away again. Not ever. I would turn around and I would fight. Every. Single. Time.

I found Scottie in the *Explore Our Solar System!* interactive exhibit. He was standing beneath a giant foam hanging model of Saturn, leaning forward, his glasses slipping down his nose, reading the placard about the planet's sixty-two moons.

"You have a girlfriend?"

He blinked at me, biding for time.

"Um," he said at last. "Yeah. Jeez—uh. Sorry."

His face was as blank and smooth as the swirling plastic surface of Saturn dangling above our heads. He wasn't just the first boy I'd ever had sex with. He was the first boy I'd ever kissed. The first boy who had ever touched me. He was all of my firsts. And he was already turning back to his placard.

Before I really even knew what I was doing I had ripped the glasses off his face, tossed them into the crater maker, and pulled the lever. And oh, what a satisfying crunch it made.

Back inside the fake space shuttle, I ran into Scottie's girlfriend's friends again, standing in front of the astronaut's toilet. It had a seat belt on it, I guess so you wouldn't float away in the middle of doing your business.

"HeybitchIheardyouletScottiedoyouinthe—"

I didn't let her finish her comment. Instead, I grabbed her by the hair and stuffed her face in the astronaut's toilet. There was no water in it—this was just a model, obviously—but when I pressed down on the flusher, it worked. It made a loud whooshing noise, and I heard her scream, and when I yanked her back up she looked dazed and terrified and one of her earlobes was bleeding pretty badly—the flusher had sucked one of her pearl studs out, torn it right through her ear.

She was rushed to the hospital to have her earlobe stitched back together, and I got kicked out of honors integrated science the next day. My counselor had nowhere else to put me, so she stuck me in basic biology, and it was boring, so

I started playing hooky, and I failed the class. I discovered that once you fail a thing and the world doesn't implode, it becomes much easier to fail everything. You realize there are worse things than failing. You realize that most of what adults try to sell you as important and necessary is really just bullshit, and that everything you always thought mattered actually kind of doesn't. By the time sophomore year started, I wasn't a nobody anymore. People knew me now, or thought they did. I had become a bottom-feeder—even Marnie kept her distance. *I don't care*, was the song inside my head the first time I had sex with a random boy I met at a party. There were no lyrics, only a chorus: *I don't care, I don't care, I don't care.*

It became the song of my whole life.

23

IT'S THE BEGINNING OF NOVEMBER, and even though red and orange leaves still cling to most of the trees, the ground is already covered with a fine layer of snow. I've discovered that my cravings for physical substances have subsided. But they've been replaced by other cravings, deeper and harder to explain, that are equally impossible to satisfy in this place. And after my shitty family therapy session, there's something I need to know.

"Why did my dad send me here?" I ask Vivian the question before she's even sat down.

She settles into her armchair, flips to a fresh page on her legal pad.

"I'm interested that you're asking me this. Do you not already know the answer to that question? Last week, you told me you were sent here because of your decision to stop lying to your dad and Alanna."

"I know, but I want to know what he *said*. Like, when he called you guys to order the transport or whatever."

"What do you think he said?"

"Can you try for once to *not* answer a question with a question?"

"Sorry," she laughs. "Bad therapist's habit."

"I guess what I want to know is, was the last straw really punching my stepmom? Or was it the other stuff?"

"What other stuff?"

"Don't play dumb. You know what I mean."

She watches me, her pen hovering above her pad of paper. I sigh.

"I just want to know if he told you about me being a slut. I mean, he's my dad, so I know he probably wouldn't say that exact word. He probably used the word on your pamphlet—'promiscuous.'"

"You're correct—he never called you a slut. I don't believe he ever would.'"

"Maybe not. But Alanna definitely would."

"What about you? Would *you* use that word—'slut'—to describe yourself, Mia?"

"The words *I* use to describe myself are irrelevant. It's the words *other* people use that matter. Or do you not understand how high school works?"

"Let's talk about that word for a minute. 'Slut.' Did you know it's almost seven hundred years old? It's probably the oldest insult in our lexicon."

"Oh God," I interrupt. "Another etymology lesson?"

"What I find funny is that the first known use of the word is from Chaucer's *The Canterbury Tales*—see? I know my dead white guys, too—and when Chaucer used it, he was describing a man. Over the years, 'slut' morphed into an insult largely directed at women. But it had nothing to do with sexuality. It was used to describe a woman who kept a messy home. Which, in the days of chamber pots and bubonic plague, was most likely pretty much any woman at all."

I sit back and relax in my chair. When Vivian's in lecture mode, it's better to just shut up and let her ramble.

"A couple hundred years after *that*, in the 1700s, the English writer Samuel Pepys used the word as a term of affection—for his own daughter, no less. 'Our little girl Susan is a most admirable Slut,' he wrote, 'and pleases us mightily.'"

I can't help myself—a laugh escapes me.

"I know, right?" Vivian laughs, too. "Poor little Susan."

"Look, I get what you're trying to say. That language is always changing and sticks and stones can break my bones but words will never hurt me. And I appreciate that. But I think we both know exactly what it means when someone calls a girl a slut in the twenty-first century."

"It's kind of a fun word to say, though," Vivian says. "When you think about it. *Slut*. Try it."

"You're weird. Slut."

"Again, but louder this time."

I roll my eyes. "*Slut*."

"Okay—now, just humor me for a minute, will you? Can you just shout that word over and over again until I tell you to stop?"

I'm curious as to where, if anywhere, this stupidity will lead, so I comply.

SLUT SLUT SLUT
SLUT SLUT SLUT
SLUT SLUT SLUT
SLUT SLUT SLUT
SLUT SLUT SLUT SLUT
SLUT SLUT SLUT SLUT
SLUT SLUT SLUT
SLUT SLUT SLUT SLUT
SLUT SLUT SLUT SLUT
SLUT SLUT SLUT SLUT SLUT
SLUT SLUT SLUT SLUT SLUT
SLUT SLUT SLUT SLUT SLUT

"Okay, okay, that's enough." Vivian laughs, holding up a hand. "Now, tell me: was there a moment in your repetition of that word where you'd said it so many times that its meaning started to break apart? When it began to feel like nothing more than a movement of your tongue and a sound coming off your mouth?"

"Yeah. Probably about the tenth or twentieth time I said it."

"Okay. Good. That's a phenomenon known as semantic satiation. Semantic satiation is the experience of saying or reading a word so many times in a row that it ceases to have any meaning. Ever since your intake, you've been asking me when you were going to get out of here and I haven't given you an answer. Now you have your answer."

"Uh . . . you've lost me."

"I want to see you grow strong enough to transcend language's ability to harm you. To take back the power to define yourself, to stop believing that other people's perceptions of you matter more than the perception you have for yourself. To stop allowing the beliefs of others to become self-fulfilling prophecies. When you have tossed 'slut' into the centrifuge and spun all its meaning away until you can see clearly the only thing that remains—the hard and true and perfect seed of who you are—*that*, Mia, will be when you're ready to go home."

24

I HAVE BEEN HERE FOR twenty-seven days. Twenty-seven days that run into each other like cars in a pileup on an otherwise empty highway. They repeat and repeat, they repeat in the sun, and again in the rain; they repeat, the days of rapidly moving clouds and the days when the morning frost has encased each individual blade of grass into a million glittering, immobile spikes of ice.

The goal of this rigidly enforced daily schedule, of the Rule of Six Inches and sewn-shut pockets, of dreary group chats where Mary Pat drones on about self-care and coping mechanisms and "adding to your mental toolboxes" while girls digest their breakfasts and daydream, of holding us accountable and teaching us responsibility in the form of scrubbing dorm toilets that smell of bleach and blood since we spend so much time together our menstrual cycles are all synced up: the goal of all this, I see now, is not to heal me but to dull my will with repetition until I've forgotten what freedom is, until I've forgotten spontaneity, danger, or adventure. Until I no longer crave these things. Until it feels like a year, or two years, so that I have to remind myself from lights-up to lights-out that it's only been twenty-seven days and I have no idea when it will end, because my therapist has given me a goal that is *holistic* and *tailored to my individual needs* and also completely impossible to ever achieve because the truth is that those girls were right, I'm trash, I'm a slut, and I can't fix it, because everything counts and I could repeat that word again and again—*"slutslutslut"*—repeat it until my voice gives way, but it won't do anything to erase the memories of what's been done to my body, of what I allowed to be done to my body by Scottie and everyone who came after him, or to change the harsh and specific timbre that laughter takes on when it's aimed directly at my life.

25

MADISON WAKES ME UP in the middle of a frigid Tuesday night and points out our window into the darkness. We see a pair of headlights coming up the drive, illuminating a soft snowfall, hear the crunch of gravel, doors opening and shutting. It's too dark to see any faces.

"Intake," whispers Madison, and just like that, I'm no longer the new girl.

We meet her in the morning at group chat. She's beautiful—like discovered-on-the-street-by-a-modeling-scout beautiful—and she seems strangely untroubled. There are no scars on her wrists; no chewed cuticles; no unfortunate, already-regretted amateur tattoos; no wild-eyed rage smoldering just behind her gaze. She doesn't even have any split ends. Most concerning? She's actually *smiling*.

We all dislike her instantly.

Mary Pat introduces her as we slouch around in our semi-circle, staring.

"Why don't you tell us a little bit about yourself, Freja?" she suggests.

"Hello, everyone." She waves a delicate hand around the room. "Like Mary Pat says, I am Freja, I am seventeen, and I am from Denmark."

"*Ooh*, an *international* student!" Madison whispers excitedly. "We haven't had one of those since Flor maturated!"

"What do we know about Freja's country?" Mary Pat smiles around the room, making brief eye contact with each of us. "Can anyone tell us where it's located?"

"The *fuck* kind of question is that? It's in fucking Europe. Do you think we're stupid, MP?"

"No, I do not." Mary Pat turns sharply and faces Trinity. "I'm simply opening up the conversation and trying to make Freja feel welcome. And frankly, I don't like your words."

Trin snort-laughs but says nothing more.

"Well, it is a small country." Freja's English is as perfect and precise as fingers tapping sharply on a keyboard, and the tiniest whisper of an accent makes it sound even more polished and sophisticated. She's wearing these shearling slippers that are a sumptuous pale pink color, like the skin of a hairless cat. "And I know children in the United States are not explicitly taught geography as part of their—"

"Denmark," I say, cutting her off. If this is the kind of Red Oak girl she's going to be, kissing Mary Pat's ass as soon as she walks through the door, then it will be necessary to put her in her place. "A peninsular Scandinavian nation, bordered on the south by Germany. Population maybe like five million? Capital: Copenhagen."

"A Viking past," continues Vera. "A socially progressive present. And perhaps it's due to the cherished Danish principle of *hygge* that those slippers of yours look cozy as fuck."

Around the semicircle, girls applaud, while Vera leans in for an air five, since slapping her hand to mine is against the Rule of Six Inches.

Mary Pat tries to lead a discussion about strategies for breaking free of negative habits of mind, but nobody even pretends to pay attention. We're all too consumed with Freja, with dissecting every detail of her: the slippers, the impeccable white Fendi tracksuit pants with the pockets neatly sewn up to make her dress code compliant, the cover-girl cheekbones, the black eyebrows microbladed to perfection, the unnervingly placid smile. Even among this assembly of rich girls, she glows with money, privilege, confidence, sophistication. Of course I couldn't care less what she thinks about *me*, but as Mary Pat drones on, I find myself tucking my own feet, clad in polka dotted rubber-bottomed Target slipper socks, beneath my chair where she can't see them.

Afterward, before morning classes begin, we convene in the common room to debrief.

"I can't even," Trinity declares, "with this snooty-ass bitch."

"Something is *off* with her," Vera says gleefully. "What was with the faux angelic smile?"

"Something's definitely rotten in the state of Denmark," I agree.

"Oh my God, nice *Hamlet* reference." Vera crumples up

her morning meditation and throws it at me. "I love that you're such a secret dork."

"But for real," Trinity continues. "Why does she *talk* like that? *I am this. She is that.* Doesn't she know how to use a contraction?"

"I *loved* her," Madison sighs. She flops down onto the gray futon and smiles dreamily up at the ceiling.

"Oh Lord. Here we go."

"Did you guys *see* her? She's *gorgeous*. And that *accent*. She almost sounds, like, *British*. But *cooler*."

"*Lord.*"

"Stop othering her, Madison," Soleil chides. "Just because someone speaks English with an accent isn't a reason to dislike them *or* like them."

"I don't like her because of her accent," Madison snaps. "I like her because of . . . because of *everything about her*." She sticks a finger in her mouth and begins dreamily tearing at a hangnail.

"*Last* thing you need," says Trinity, "is another stalking victim. You're on track to get out of here this spring, once you can stop picking at your damn self for a minute."

"I *told* you guys, I have a thing with *impulse* cont—"

Just then, Freja glides past the doorway in her velvet cat-flesh slippers and we all fall silent, listening to the *chuff chuff chuff* of her feet against the linoleum, consumed in our own private thoughts about her, about ourselves.

26

THAT NIGHT, AT DINNER, I'm sitting at my regular Birchwood crew's table when Freja brings over her tray. She doesn't ask if she can sit with us. She just sits. Which might not seem like a big deal, since our student body is way too small and full of misfits for people to clique up like they do at a regular high school. But it goes totally against unspoken Red Oak etiquette. Freja lives in Conifer, and the normal thing to do, especially when you're new, is to sit with the other girls in your house.

"I like your earrings," Madison says hopefully as soon as she sits down.

This is obviously not true. The earrings are giant geometric gold hoops, twinkling off the track lighting, brushing against Freja's soft, sloping shoulders. They are far too on trend for Madison's hopelessly preppy aesthetic.

"Thank you, Madison," Freja says, tossing her glossy blackbird-wing hair. "These are my mother's."

"Well, you know what they say." Trinity half stands, leans over our hunks of meat loaf and clots of mashed potatoes, and flicks one of Freja's earrings. "The bigger the hoop, the bigger the ho."

While we all fall over each other laughing, the hoop trembles and shakes and dances on Freja's earlobe. She reaches up coolly and stills it with two tapered fingers.

"No," she says, staring into Trinity's eyes. "I did not know this is what they say."

"Don't pay any attention to Trinity," Madison says quickly. "We're all *super* happy you're here."

"Speaking of," Vera says, her voice syrupy with malice, "why *are* you here, sweetie?"

"Ah." Freja looks around at each of us and takes a delicate bite of her meat loaf. "So this is the question you were all whispering about today."

"We weren't whispering," I say. "Anyone at this table will say anything to anyone's face. Try us."

Freja blinks calmly at me. Her napkin is folded across her lap like she's dining at the Four Seasons or something. "Very well. Do you know of a Nicoline Pedersen?"

"I mean," says Madison, "I feel like the name sounds *familiar*? But, like, I can't exactly *place* it?"

"She is my mother."

"Madison's just being nice," Vera says. "Don't flatter yourself, honey. None of us has any clue who your mother is."

"Well," Freja says, returning to her meat loaf, "then that is why I am here."

27

IF WE LIVED IN THE WORLD, we could simply google Nicoline Pedersen and we would be able to at least partially figure out Freja's deal. But as Vera likes to say, we don't live in the world: we live in Red Oak. So we can't figure out a damn thing, and it's driving us crazy.

I haven't been here long enough to have even the faintest shot at supervised tech privileges, and Vera and Trinity skipped out on toilet duty last week, so they're a no-go, too. Which leaves Madison. Problem is, Mary Pat won't let her have even one minute of supervised internet time unless she can keep her teeth away from her hands for long enough to at least let them scab up.

And then Trinity gets an idea. She has her dad FedEx over a half gallon of children's bubbles and a long plastic wand.

"For those oral fixations of yours," she says, handing the bottle over to Madison after Dee has sniffed and tasted the contents to make sure it's not filled with, like, soap-flavored vodka or something. "It helped my dad quit smoking."

We're all skeptical about the bubbles, even Mary Pat, but would you believe it? It actually works. Over the next four days, Madison manages to keep her hands almost completely out of her mouth. All day long she's blowing bubbles, and even though every time I try to talk to her, I feel like I'm stuck in either a rave or a preschool class, by day five, skin— actual dermis—is growing over her tormented hands.

"MP, you should put me on salary," Trinity tells Mary Pat, as we all gather round to examine the delicate scabs that haven't yet been gnawed or torn or picked off by Madison's extreme BFRBs. She even takes to wearing her wig to bed at night, even though it's hot and itchy, to combat the temptation to pull out her hair. And Mary Pat keeps her word: she awards Madison ten chaperoned minutes of computer time. No social media is allowed, of course, and no email, either; last time she was given *that* privilege, Vera reports, she sent a thirty-two-page love letter to her ex-girlfriend. ("In her defense," Vera said, "it was mostly Billie Eilish lyrics.")

But she can use Google, and, that afternoon, with Dee hovering behind her, Madison manages to stick to her task.

We gather in the common room during constructive relaxation to listen to her findings.

"Nicoline Pedersen," Madison begins, reading from the notes she's taken in her journal. "Or, more commonly, 'Nic,' is a pop star and reality-television host known affectionately by some as 'the Beyoncé of Denmark.'"

"Blasphemy!" shouts Vera. "There is only *one* Beyoncé."

"Denmark is like a hundred times smaller than the United States," I say. "So that means that even if she *is* the Beyoncé of Denmark, she's still only, like, one one-hundredth of *our* Beyoncé."

"I find your centering of American culture problematic." Soleil yawns.

"Well, I find your decentering of Beyoncé even *more* problematic."

"It doesn't matter," sighs Vera. "Even a .001 Beyoncé is still like a thousand times greater than a regular person."

"Okay, so her mom's famous," Trinity says. "So what? It's not like she's the first celebrity kid to come to Red Oak. It doesn't tell us what she's doing *here*."

"That's true," Madison agrees. "Didn't Olivia once pawn her dad's Super Bowl ring for drugs?"

"Rings. Plural."

"Come *on*, Madison. Didn't you dig up any good dirt on this chick?"

"Not really, honestly."

"You didn't get distracted scrolling through Google images of her, did you?"

"No! Except . . . well, she was at this film premiere last year, and oh my God, she was wearing this Balmain gown with these like chains on it and I googled how much it cost and it was, like, *twenty thousand*—"

Trinity and Vera simultaneously pick up the couch cushions and throw them at her.

"Madison, you're hopeless," says Trinity. "Vera, we're just

going to have to take this matter into our own hands."

"Yep." Vera reaches over to pop the perfectly round bubble Madison has just floated across the common room. "Never send in a girl to do a woman's job."

28

OUR PE TEACHER, Coach Leslie, is this extremely fit former college hockey star with a plume of extremely white hair and a mouthful of extremely white teeth who swigs spring water from a gallon jug and looks as likely to don a high heel or ingest a mind-altering substance as I am to run for class president. If an organic granola bar somehow became sentient, it would take the form of Coach Leslie. Her motto for guiding us toward maturation, she often shouts at us, is HEAL:

Hiking!

Exercise!

Air!

Laughter!

Which is why, even though the ground is already covered with a muddy layer of snow, she often leads us on nature hikes[22] through the walking trails while cracking a series of knock-knock jokes that are too pitiful to repeat here. On one such hike a couple days after Freja's arrival,

---

[22] Or "death marches," as Vera, who is not big on physical fitness, calls them.

Vera and Trinity take the opportunity to flank her at the back of the line.

"Okay," Vera says. "Your mom's famous. So what?"

Freja shrugs, her Saint Laurent fur boots squelching through muddy slush. "So nothing."

"Look." Trinity steps in front of her on the trail. "Everybody's in here for a reason, okay? I put naked pictures of myself all over the internet and cost my mom her seat in Congress. Vera here is a self-harmer."

"Don't forget formerly suicidal!" Vera adds brightly.

"Madison tried to kill her ex-girlfriend, Soleil's a junkie, Mia beat up her stepmom, Swizzie's a compulsive liar, Charlotte has anger management issues, et cetera. And don't even get me started on our *backstories*. My point is, we're all on the same level, okay? And we just want to know why *you're* here."

"And we'll find out one way or another," Vera says, stepping with casual aggression into Freja's personal space, "so you might as well just tell us."

Freja smiles pleasantly from one girl to the next as she climbs over a fallen tree. "But you see, girls, there is no reason I am here."

"Don't think you're better than us, sweetheart." Vera's voice has oiled itself into a growl. "It's like Trinity said: *everyone's* here for a reason."

"Very well." Freja stops to turn and face them. "Here is

the reason: my mother, she wanted to send me to boarding school in the US. I have family in Minneapolis, so she has chosen to send me here. This is why I am here."

"Wait." Vera holds up a mittened hand. "Are you trying to say that your mom sent you to Red Oak thinking it was just a normal American boarding school with, like, normal preppy American kids?"

"This is correct."

Trinity and Vera bug their eyes at each other and burst out laughing so hysterically that a startled spruce grouse shoots out of some nearby bushes and takes off squawking into the trees.

"That's right, gals!" shouts Coach Leslie, waving her walking stick from the front of the line. "Laughing feels *good*, but let's try to respect the peace and quiet of nature while we release those yummy endorphins, okay?"

Vera, laughing even harder now, calls out an apology, first to Coach Leslie, then to the spruce grouse, which has already disappeared back into the forest and presumably can't hear her anyway.

"Oh, now I have heard it all," Trinity says, wiping her eyes with her gloves. "Now I have heard it *all*."

"She thought she was going to get up here and take some AP classes, maybe try out for the field hockey team or some shit?" Vera shakes her head as she kicks through a patch of melting ice. "You poor thing, Freja. Well, once you hop on that family therapy session at the end of week two, hopefully you can convince 'Nic' to get you the hell out of here."

"No." Freja smiles calmly. "You do not understand me. I knew what this place was. My mother did not—her English is not very good. But mine is."

"Wait." Vera stops so short I nearly crash into her. "You're telling me you didn't have to be here—that you're here *by choice*?"

"Yes."

"Lies," sings Trinity. "Lies, lies, lies."

"You may choose to believe me, or you may choose not to believe me," Freja says, picking over a muddy puddle in her sumptuous fur boots. "In Copenhagen, I had bodyguards. I could not leave my house without being swarmed. I had photographers in my face, all the time. I could not have boyfriends; I could not even have friends. I could not be normal. Here, there are no phones, no tabloid stories filled with gossip. And you have all been so awful to me—so cruel! And this makes me so happy!"

Happy? We all look at each other, confused.

"No one has ever been cruel to me in my life! They are all too busy—what is the English phrase? Sucking my ass?"

That does it. Vera and Trinity collapse into the shallow snow, screeching with laughter. Three more terrified spruce grouses go clapping up into the sky, and Coach Leslie, who has finally realized they are laughing at something other than her dumb jokes, orders the two of them back to campus to wash dishes.

29

IT'S BEEN A WEEK since Freja's arrival, and for most of us, the new girl has settled into nothing more than a curiosity—beautiful, yeah, and famous, supposedly, but not particularly funny, cool, smart, or interesting. We're all just glad she lives in Conifer so we don't have to hang around her that much.

All of us, that is, except Madison.

When she's on kitchen duty, she makes a giant Rice Krispies treat in the shape of a heart and presents it to Freja after dinner.

During group chat, she openly stares at Freja with such naked ardor that Mary Pat has to remind her that sometimes you can violate someone's personal space without ever actually touching them.

"So now I'm not even allowed to *look* at people?" we heard her whining when Mary Pat kept her after the session for a one-on-one and we all stood around the door, eavesdropping. "Even the way I *look* at people is problematic now?"

A hushed response from Mary Pat.

And then an impassioned cry from Madison: "What are you gonna do, put one of those cones around my neck that they put on dogs to stop them from licking their wieners?" which sent us all running down the hall, dying with laughter.

During homework hours, she quietly hums songs from Lana Del Rey's *Born to Die* album and stares off into space with tragic longing.

In foreign language independent study, she puts aside her usual French and signs up for a Duolingo program in Danish.

One night, at dinner, Freja makes the innocent mistake of complimenting Madison's glasses. Madison immediately yanks them off her face and holds them out to Freja. "You want them, they're yours," she says. "They're real Kate Spade."

"Oh, no, no, no," laughs Freja. "I was only saying that they are nice, Madison."

"*Here.*" Madison shakes them in Freja's face. "They're yours. Please. Take them. I want you to have them. They'll look so much better on you than they do on me, anyway."

We all expect Freja to wave her away again—this is a girl who owns a twenty-thousand dollar Balmain dress, after all, so what does she need with other people's hand-me-downs?— but instead she arches a sculpted eyebrow.

"Are you sure these are Kate Spade?"

"*Positive.* I swear. I picked them out myself at Pearle Vision!"

"Very well, then." Freja accepts the glasses, examines

them, then slips them on. "These are very strong, no?" She squints around the table. "You are sure you do not need them?"

Madison blinks, her blue, weepy, mostly lashless eyes filling with tears at the glory of seeing something of hers adorning Freja's face. "I'm positive," she says. "I have a backup pair."

"Those old pink ones?" asks Vera. "Aren't those from like sixth grade?"

"You can barely see out of those!" exclaims Trinity.

"They're fine," insists Madison. "Really. Freja—those look *amazing* on you. I'd be honored if you kept them."

And Freja, to *our* amazement—and annoyance—agrees. She thanks Madison, slips them into the front pocket of her backpack, then gets up to return her tray to the serving line.

"What is *wrong* with you?" Trinity's voice is filled with disgust, but Madison just smiles dreamily, watching Freja scrape her leftover potpie into the garbage.

Later that night, after lights-out, Madison, in her outdated pink glasses, crashes into a wall on her way to the bathroom, chipping a tooth, and even though she cries about it, nobody feels sorry for her dumb ass.

30

IT'S NOT EVEN THANKSGIVING YET, but the stream outside Vivian's office has frozen solid. Snowdrifts are blown halfway up her window, obscuring most of the view and making her tiny space feel even more claustrophobic than usual.

"So," she says, crossing her legs and peering at me over her reading glasses.

"So," I say.

"How are you?"

"Fine. I think I have seasonal affective disorder."

She looks at me. "Have you been feeling down lately? Sad? Dark thoughts? That kind of thing?"

"I was *joking*. I'm just sick of winter, that's all."

"Well, you're going to need to get used to it, because technically it's still autumn."

"I hate east-central Minnesota."

"Yes, so you've mentioned. Let me try asking you again: how are you?"

I reach back to tighten my ponytail, adjust myself in my chair. "You want to know, honestly?"

"Of course."

"Well, I'm frustrated."

"With anyone or anything in particular?"

"Why, since you asked: you."

"Me? Why's that?"

"Because why am I even *here* right now?"

"Mia. Come on." Vivian wiggles her pen between her fingers, which is what she always does when she's annoyed with me. "You've got to start focusing on your current reality, on the goals we've set for you, and get over this fixation that you don't belong at Red Oak."

"No, I don't even mean that. I mean, why am I specifically *here*? Sitting in this chair, in this office, with you?"

She just looks at me with her tell-me-more face.

"I've been coming to see you twice a week for over a month now and you still haven't really asked me about anything important."

"Really? Like what?"

"Um, I don't know, like my mom? And the fact that she got murdered?"

"Do you *want* me to ask you about your mom?"

"It's not that I *want* you to. It's just that I've been going to one therapist or another since she died, which is pretty much as long as my working memory goes back, and every single one of them is always dying to talk about her."

"I was made to understand that you don't remember your mother."

"I *don't*."

"Well, then, when your other therapists have asked about her, what did you say?"

"I don't know. Nothing. They do most of the talking."

"And they say . . . ?"

"The usual."

"What's the usual?"

"Well, the most recent ones have told me that I have a mother-shaped void in my life, which I'm trying to numb with drugs or fill with boys."

"Huh."

"And that it won't work because the drugs are temporary and the boys are the wrong shape."

"Ah."

"But here's my question: if the void in my life is mother-shaped, and I only had one mother, then aren't I doomed to have that void unfilled forever?"

"I suppose you are."

"So I might as well just do whatever the hell I want because I'll never feel whole anyway."

"I suppose that's one way of looking at it—though I would add, with respect, that not every kid who loses a parent ends up making some of the choices you've made. I don't say this as a rebuke. I say it to remind you that—and we've talked about this—even though you experienced a catastrophic loss at a young age, it shouldn't dictate the remainder of your life.

You don't want your mother's death to become a crutch."

"A *crutch*?"

"A catch-all excuse for why you make the choices you make."

"I don't do that *at all*. My dad and Alanna and my teachers are the ones who blame every bad thing I do on my dead mom."

"Well, why do *you* think you behave the way you do?"

"I don't know, maybe because I'm just kind of an asshole? Does there have to be a *reason*?"

"Well, yes, there usually does. Especially because you're *not*, at least in my estimation, an asshole."

"Aw. Thanks, Viv."

"There are behaviors, and then there are issues. If you can get to the issue, you can start to change the behavior."

"Please," I say flatly. "Tell me more."

"Well, since you brought it up," she says, referring back to her notes and ignoring my sarcasm, "let's talk about some of your behaviors. Those void-filling boys, I mean. Starting with Xander. That's the boy you were seeing when you—"

"We weren't *seeing* each other."

"Okay. Let's forget about labels. Was this a boy you cared about?"

"No."

"And yet you were intimate with him."

"That's one way of putting it."

"And the other boys—did you care for any of them?"

"Some more than others." I look out the window at the whitewashed landscape. "But at the end of the day . . . no, not really. And they didn't care about me, either."

"So if you didn't care about them, and you don't feel they cared about you—why do you think you kept doing it?"

"I don't know. Because it was fun?"

"You know, Mia, some cognitive psychiatrists believe that humans are often unconsciously drawn to the repetition of painful experiences."

"What are you even talking about? I just told you it was fun. Who said anything about pain?"

"Forgive me. Maybe I'm misunderstanding you. Are you saying the sex with these boys, Xander and the others, was satisfying?"

"What do you mean *satisfying*?"

"Physically. Emotionally. Did the sex make you feel good?"

"Yeah." I clear my throat. "Definitely. Otherwise why would I bother?"

"Wow. That's great. Especially because it's very unusual for women—especially very young women, like yourself—to experience orgasm with a partner when there's no real intimacy there. And it's nearly *impossible* to experience orgasm when you're under the influence of drugs or alcohol, which you often were, when you engaged in these sex acts. Correct?"

"*Correct*, but that other part you said—that's bullshit."

"What other part?"

"The idea that a girl can't enjoy sex unless she's in love. Unless there are candles and negligees and silk sheets and sensual jazz music playing and shit like that."

"Have you ever given any thought to what *you* like, Mia? What *you* want in a romantic encounter? Because what you just described —the negligees, the candles—that sounds to me like a cross between a Hallmark movie and a porn film."

Her words summon a memory into my mind. Dillon Keating. LaBagh Woods at the height of summer, mosquitoes buzzing our bodies and my back pressing into the warm soft moss. Far away, the sound of laughter. He'd yanked my underwear down my thighs so fast that it tore in half. *I saw a guy do that in a porn once*, he said. *I didn't think it would actually work.* We both had laughed then, me the loudest, so he knew I was cool with it, that I wasn't scared at all. Black cherry vodka and flat Sprite in plastic cups spilled near our heads and fizzed into the mud. I'd only meant to kiss him.

"You know what?" I say. "I'd rather talk about my dead mother than talk about this."

31

THANKSGIVING IS A HOLIDAY that's all about family and food, so spending it away from your family is always going to suck, no matter how good the food is.

And I'll admit: the food is good. Madison, Freja, and some of the other Conifer girls have spent all week in the kitchen with Chef Lainie, blind-baking pie crusts, tearing up stale bread for stuffing, mixing and plastic-wrapping cranberry sauce, and brining three massive turkeys freshly slaughtered and shipped from a poultry farm up in Pequot Lakes. The rest of us non–Martha Stewart types have been kept busy with chores like cleaning windows, dusting drapes, washing baseboards, and vacuuming the dorm hallways.

On Thanksgiving afternoon, we all help push the tables together in the middle of the cafeteria to make one long banquet-hall-type setup, with an elaborate cornucopia centerpiece Madison fashioned out of leaves and sticks she'd gathered along the walking trails. Outside the big picture windows, the snow falls, fine as cake flour. There is a hot chocolate station[23] next to the salad bar; homemade pump-kin, Dutch apple, and chocolate mousse pies; stuffing made with sofrito and torn sourdough and decadent dollops of butter; bowls of cranberry relish, cranberry chutney, and cranberry salad; trimmed green beans; brussels sprouts with candied bacon; the three huge local turkeys, golden and crispy-skinned; and, of course, because this is Minnesota, a large assortment of Hot Dishes. When we walk into the cafeteria to sit down for dinner, it doesn't smell like a school cafeteria anymore. It smells like a *home*. Which is maybe why, halfway through our meal, Madison puts her fork down crossways on her plate, just like her well-born mother taught her, and begins to cry. This unleashes a domino effect across the table, with the exception of me and Vera, who simply roll our eyes at each other and split an extra helping of popovers. Still, it's hard to have fun when everybody around you is sob-bing, homemade popovers notwithstanding.

"Don't despair, everyone," Mary Pat says with her sig-nature brand of willful positivity as she helps herself to a second serving of mashed potatoes and all around her, girls press their napkins to their eyes. "After we clean up here and put dishes away, I have a surprise for all of you!"

Mary Pat isn't big on surprises. She's big on structure, routine, and boundaries. So we all begin chattering excitedly

---

[23] Manned by Dee, who stands by stoically holding a whipped cream can, doling out a squirt to those who want it, lest any of us try to make off with the whole can for a quick huff in the dorm bathrooms.

among ourselves, trying to guess what the surprise might be. Trinity thinks it's going to be like what they do on reality TV, when they have contestants' family members squirreled away somewhere, and that any minute now, our parents and brothers and sisters are going to come strolling through the front door of the cafeteria. Swizzie thinks it's going to be some sort of field trip, maybe to Mille Lacs to see the holiday lights. Soleil wonders if it's going to be a cheat day, where Mary Pat allows us one hour to do whatever drug we want.

"A girl can dream, anyway," she says.

Of course it turns out to be none of these things. After we've stuffed ourselves, cleared the table, packed the leftovers into giant Tupperware containers, and washed the dishes, Mary Pat and Coach Leslie march us through the snow, across the quad, and over to the rec center. Mary Pat unlocks the gym and throws open the double doors with a flourish.

"Ta-da!" She sweeps her arms to reveal a stack of shoeboxes piled up in the middle of the gym floor.

"You got us . . . new shoes?" somebody asks. "*That's* the surprise?"

"Not exactly! Go take a look, girls! Find your size! Happy Thanksgiving!"

"I have wide feet," says Ariadne, a Wiccan-identifying redhead who lives in Conifer. "And fallen arches. I really can't be expected to wear mass-produced—"

"Oh my *God*!" shrieks Madison, who has just lifted the lid off a box of size nines. "They're *figure* skates!" She lifts the pristine white boots reverently from their bed of tissue paper and hugs them to her chest. She squints joyfully around at us from behind her outdated pink glasses. "I used to skate competitively when I was a kid! I gave it up in sixth grade when I couldn't land my axel, but still . . . Oh, I *love* skating!"

"What'd you do, Mary Pat," says Trin, skeptically approaching the stack, "rob a truck?"

"They're from an anonymous donor," Mary Pat says, tossing her a box. "They're all brand-new!"

"Are they ours to keep?"

"Well, yes and no." She clears her throat. "They'll have to be kept here in the gym. Safety purposes."

"Suicide by ice skate," says Vera, lifting a boot out of its wrapping and pretending to slice her throat with its blade. "Just imagine the headlines."

"Really, Vera." Mary Pat pinches the bridge of her nose. "Is that necessary?"

"Is this mandatory?" asks Bronwynne, our other Conifer Wiccan. "Because I have conscientious objections to organized sports."

"I'm from Southern California," says Soleil. "What do *I* know about ice-skating?"

"I, too," adds Freja, "have no experience with this sport."

"But *I* can teach you, Freja!"

Freja's face pinches up with the faintest hint of distaste at Madison's proposition. "You do not need—"

"I can teach *all* you guys! My old coach used to say that figure skating is like riding a bike—you might be a bit wobbly at first, but once you get the hang of it, it's a skill you'll have forever!"

"Madison, I think you'll make a wonderful coach," Mary Pat says with a smile. She points at those of us who are slouched sullenly against the mat-covered gym wall. "This is going to be *fun*, girls. Okay?" She looks around at each of us, her face stretching with the intensity of her smile. "*Okay?*"

"Do me a favor," Vera whispers over to me, testing the sharpness of her toe pick with the pad of her finger and drawing a drop of dark blood in the process. "If I ever become that earnest about *anything*, take me out into the woods and leave me to the fucking wolves."

32

THE WEATHER OVER Thanksgiving weekend is fine and cold and bright, and despite our initial hesitations, we spend almost the whole of it on the ice. As we practice, members of our weekend staff sit on the log near the shore to cheer us on. Mary Pat, in particular, observes us with such satisfaction that I'm half convinced the "anonymous donor" is Madison's mom and that this whole thing is just an elaborate plan her parents hatched with the Red Oak staff to help promote her self-confidence and get her maturated by the spring, cured and healthy, just in time for junior prom.

It's cool to see this side of Madison, though. Off the ice, she's still an awkward hand-eating weirdo, but when she laces up her skates it's like she morphs into this different person, this *athlete*, who instinctively knows how to move her body through the world. Watching her glide forward and backward, showing off her spins, teaching us the names of each: the scratch, the change-foot, the layback, the sit, the camel— it's a nice reminder that everybody's got more inside them than you can ever see at first look, and that some of the time, people can surprise you in a *good* way.

Like most of the other girls here, I was never much of a sports kid myself. Well, that's not exactly true: I played soccer in elementary school. I loved it, and I wasn't terrible at it, either. But the problem is, when you're a kid, sports are just sports, and you can play them for the simple and wonderful reason that they're fun. But when you get to high school, sports become more than sports; they become connected to identity, baked into the ecosystem of your social world, a signifier for other people for how to place you. By the time spring soccer tryouts came around freshman year, I'd already been branded—the slut who seduced a senior girl's boyfriend, who gets drunk at parties, who gets high, who gives blow jobs to near-strangers. Girls like that don't play *soccer*. Everybody knows that, so what was the point in even trying out? Now I wonder, as I circle Lake Onamia, practicing my wobbly, new-found skills, could my entire shitstorm of a high school career have been avoided if I'd just shown up on the practice field that rainy March afternoon instead of going over to Marnie's to steal weed gummies from her arthritic grandma? What if I had made the team? Maybe the discipline of all those early morning practices, the accountability to my teammates and coach, the need to pay close attention to what I was putting into my body . . . maybe all those things would have kept me honest. Kept me good—maybe even good enough to reclassify me in the social hierarchy. I could have been jock identifying. I could have been a fresh-cheeked good girl with French-braided pigtails threaded through with school colors. Muscled legs encased in swishy pants and Adidas slides with socks. Team spaghetti dinners prepared at somebody's house by somebody's mom. Taylor Swift–soundtracked bus rides to all-state tournaments. Chaste, sober parties with the freshman boys' team.

I guess Vivian has a point about how I've allowed other people's opinions of me to become self-fulfilling prophecies: maybe if I had just shown up for those stupid tryouts, I never would have ended up here.

But, I mean, there's not a whole lot I can do about it now, except to skate around the lake until my legs burn, until I remember that I can still use my body the way I once used it when I was a kid: for the singular purpose of my very own pleasure.

33

"I'D LOVE TO PICK UP where we left off before the holiday," says Vivian at our Monday session.

"Where'd we leave off again?" I stretch out my legs, wonderfully sore from my weekend on skates.

"We were talking about whether you'd had emotionally and physically satisfying sexual relationships with your partners."

"Oh, yes. Now I remember. And I said I'd rather talk about my dead mom than talk about my sex life with you."

"But, Mia, if you don't talk to me, then I can't help you. And if I can't help you, then I can't track your growth. And if I can't track your growth—"

"—then you can't maturate me, and I will be stuck here until I die of boredom or turn eighteen, whichever comes first?"

Vivian simply smiles at me.

"Fine." I sit back in my chair, pull my aching legs to my chest. "What do you want to know?"

"Thank you." She picks up her pen. "Why don't we start at the beginning?"

"The beginning?"

I'm good at pretending to be dumb and not know what people are talking about—I did a lot of this in elementary school, when I was trying to blend in as just normal smart, not weird smart. Vivian, of course, knows that I'm just stalling.

"Yes. The beginning. Why don't you tell me about your first sexual experience, Mia?"

"Ugh. Fine. His name was Scottie. He was an older guy."

"How much older?"

"Oh, not, like inappropriately older. He was a senior; I was a freshman."

"So you were, what, fourteen? Fifteen?"

"Fourteen."

"Ah. That's pretty young, huh?"

"I mean . . . it's not *that* young." I glance up at her. "Is it?"

"Well, it's a lot younger than eighteen."

"He might have been seventeen. He didn't tell me when his fucking birthday was. We didn't trade, like, astrological signs."

"Do you want to tell me about it?"

"There's not much to tell. The whole thing was about ten minutes from start to finish."

"So it shouldn't take too long for you to tell me about it."

"Yeah, but I just—don't want to. Why don't you give me another one of your boring etymology lectures instead? That's what I'm in the mood for."

"Mia," she says gently. "You've got to let me help you."

I read her kindness act as a threat: *Either open up to me, or you ain't going nowhere, kid.* And so, because I can't imagine lasting a whole winter here without going Jack-Nicholson-in-*The-Shining* level stir crazy, I relent. I tell her the story, the whole story, of me and Scottie Curry and the things that came after, and I even cry a little bit because I figure maybe she'll take my tears as a sign of sincerity, that I'm really doing the emotional work. When I'm done talking, she hands me a tissue.

"Mia," she says. "Did you ever tell an adult about what happened between you and Scottie?"

I let out a dry, barky laugh. "Who, like my dad? Because that wouldn't be awkward at all."

"Mia, I know you're trying to be flip about this. But I'm here to tell you: your experience wasn't typical."

"Ah. I should have had the jazz music and the silk sheets, huh?"

"Mia." She balances her notepad on her lap, then reaches across the space between us to take my two hands in hers. I look down, doubtfully, at her fingers wrapped around mine.

"Uh—did you forget about the Rule of Six Inches, Viv?"

"Mia," she says again. "What you just described to me: that's sexual assault. Scottie assaulted you."

"Sexual *assault*? As in, *rape*?"

She nods. I yank my hands away from her.

"Oh my God. Here we go. Look, I'm not some fucking *victim*, okay?"

"Rape isn't just something that happens to girls in alleys with strangers."

"God, Vivian. Did you listen to a word I said? *I* made the first move; *I* dressed up for him. I *thought* 'stop,' but never bothered to *say* 'stop.' That's not rape. That's just a freshman idiot girl doing idiot things and getting exactly what she deserves in the process."

"Did he ever ask you if you wanted to do what you were doing?"

"I kissed him first! Of course he thought I wanted it!"

"Did he ever ask if it was okay? If *you* were okay? Did you say that word, 'yes,' ever?"

"No, but—"

"An older boy in a position of relative power invited you to his empty home, had sex with you despite your utter silence and clear discomfort, and then afterward stood by silently and allowed you to be bullied and mocked, allowed your life to fall apart, and he never spoke to you again. He assaulted you, Mia. And he left you, alone, to bear the consequences. Think about the repercussions this has had in your life. And then the repercussions—if any—it's had in his."

"This is the dumbest shit I've ever heard. You're trying to tell me I was raped and I didn't even know it. I'm not fucking *stupid*, Vivian."

"No, you're not stupid. You just— Let me put it this way. So, at the start of World War II, the Jewish philosopher and journalist Raymond Aron fled his home in Paris. He moved to London and joined the Free French forces. Years later, when asked whether he'd understood the evils the Nazis were committing against his people back on the European continent, he said: 'I knew, but I didn't believe it. And because I didn't believe it, I didn't know.'"

"I don't want one of your stupid history lessons right now."

"Scottie raped you, Mia. This is something you've always known. You just didn't want to believe it. And because you didn't want to believe it, you didn't know."

Whore.

Slut.

Pig.

Cum dumpster.

White trash.

Punch line.

Warm hole.

If words can reach a saturation point, where you say them so many times they cease to have meaning, then maybe bodies can, too. If I share my body with enough people, it ceases to belong to me. It belongs to the world and the world can do what it wants with this body that was once mine.

Whore. Slut. Pig. Cum dumpster. White trash. Punch line. Warm hole.

Whoreslutpigcumdumpsterwhitetrashpunchlinewarmhole

whoreslutpigcumdumpsterwhitetrashpunchlinewarmholewhoreslut
pigcumdumpsterwhitetrashpunchlinewarm—

"Deep breaths," I hear Vivian's voice, muffled, coming from somewhere. My head is in my lap, my hands are pressed over my ears, and I can't breathe, but at least no one is touching me.

"Deep breaths. From your belly. Deep breaths from your belly."

But I can't—

I can't seem to—

"Your life doesn't need to be—"

What's wrong with me?

"Your life doesn't—"

Why am I so—

"Your life—"

Why am I like this? Why didn't somebody tell me there are no trial runs; that everything you do in your life counts; that you can drink or smoke enough to forget what you did and what was done to you but you can't do anything to forget the way it made you feel?

"Allow yourself to imagine something better. "

But—

"Something that is deserving of who you are. Something better than what you've had."

But—

"And then forgive yourself for the mistakes that came afterward. Forgive yourself and let it go."

34

I DON'T SLEEP WELL.

I feel that word—"rape"—like a small, cruel animal, hunched and pressing on my chest all night. Maybe if I shouted it enough times, I could destroy it, but the shape of that one syllable feels dirty in my mouth, and anyway, I don't want to wake Madison, who's been sleeping like a champ ever since she started her skating program.

The next afternoon, which is both brilliantly sunny and cold as fuck, Coach Leslie marches us out to the lake for PE, and it's just the wake-up call I need. Out here, it's so frigid that my eyes won't stop leaking and my skin vibrates. The cold floats up from the frozen water, snaking up my legs and into my head like a full body shot of espresso. My brain itself feels like a rough ice sculpture, with sharp thoughts carving into it, clear and potent. One such thought: I'm glad I'm here, at least for now. My life at Red Oak is as rigidly choreographed as a symphony. There are no variables, no x. I do not have choices anymore. But here's the tradeoff, and I surprise myself by considering that maybe it's a fair one: at least I know I'm safe here.

All of us, even the sports-averse Wiccans from Conifer, can now wobble our way from one end of the lake to the other without making total clowns of ourselves. Madison, meanwhile, has been meeting Coach Leslie on the ice during constructive relaxation to practice her jumps, and today she unveils them for us—the salchow, the toe loop, and the lutz. As she spins and leaps across the surface of the lake, we reward her, after each perfect landing, with raucous applause.

"They're just singles," she says shyly, but her eyes shine with exertion and pleasure. "It's not a big deal."

That's when Freja suggests that Madison try her axel, the jump she could never land, that brought her skating days to an end.

"If you can do all these other jumps, Madison," Freja says, "why can you not do this one?"

Nodding, whoops of agreement from both Birchwood and Conifer and the staff gathered on the log.

"You guys don't get it." Madison's hands wave before her mouth as she turns in nervous little swizzles up and down the ice. "An axel is the only jump that takes off going forward. It's like a whole thing with physics."

"Perhaps," says Freja, "it has never been a problem of physics but of confidence."

"No, but, like, it's really hard, even if it doesn't look it. And I could never land it because I'm too heavy. If I had more of a skater's body—"

"Your body is beautiful," Freja says simply. "What is

wrong with your body?"

"You think my body is beautiful?" Madison's hands, ever fluttering, still themselves against her heart.

I'm afraid for a moment that she might faint.

"Yes. It is a strong body. A healthy body." Freja puts her hands firmly on her hips. "You will do this axel for us."

Somebody in Conifer starts the chant: "Mad-i-*son*! Mad-i-*son*!" And everybody joins in, but our cheers aren't really necessary. It is Freja who has decreed that Madison will do her axel, and for Madison, Freja's opinion is the only one that matters.

"Confidence," she says slowly. "You're right. I mean, skating is more of a mental sport than people realize. If I *believe* I can do it . . ."

"*Exactly*. Then you can do it."

We move out of the way, gather in a crowd at the shore of the frozen lake to give her enough space. Madison bites her lip, and a glaze comes over her eyes, so that her face is frozen into a facade of pure grit. She is clenching her teeth, pumping her arms, building momentum. Whistling past us, her arms reach up, her leg swings out like the hand of a clock, and then she is airborne, tight and spinning, an arc, a calculation, across the sky. I don't say this lightly: she is magnificent.

She turns her leg out, preparing for her landing, but even I, a person who knows next to nothing about ice-skating, can see there isn't enough room between the sky and the ground, she has overshot it, and she hits the ice hip-first, a jarring crash that sets my teeth clacking. Something skids across the surface of the lake, then, and at first I think it's a bird, maybe a spruce grouse startled by the crash, before I realize that it's her wig, which has come free of its hairpins during the impact and is skidding away across the slicked plane of Lake Onamia.

Now, sure.

I suppose what happened is objectively funny. People falling is funny. People losing a wig as they fall on their ass is probably hilarious.

Except that it's Madison. Madison, with her hard-won, newborn pride. Who picks and plucks and squeezes and scratches at every surface of herself, making manifest the torture of anxiety-ridden thoughts, who is convinced that she's ugly and picks at herself as a way to cope with this conviction, then feels even uglier because she's picked at herself, like one distorted mirror across from another distorted mirror, reflecting self back on to ruined self, on and on into infinity. Madison, who for one hopeful moment believed Freja, that possessing the thing you want the most is a simple matter of confidence. And for people like Freja, who are born into a world and a body that reassures them at every turn that they deserve every good thing they've ever gotten, maybe it is. But Madison is different. Which is why you can tease her, you can prod her, you can mock her with a mix of exasperation and affection—we all do it, all the time—but you can never, ever laugh at Madison.

Doesn't everyone know that?

Does Freja really not know that?

Her regal laughter bubbles out into the flinty, clear, cold air, shatters against Madison like a body blow. Vera skates off to retrieve the wig while I go over to help Madison up. She knocks my arm away, rolls over onto her hands and knees and stands up slowly, holding on to her hip. Coach Leslie is skating out to us, in long, clean strides that remind us she once played elite hockey.

And Freja is still laughing.

She's doubled over with it, not seeming to notice that nobody else is joining in. Madison looks around wildly. The grit is gone from her face and she is once again herself, skating with shaky, ungainly strides toward the edge of the lake where we've piled our boots and coats. She is kicking off her skates, shoving her socked feet back into her snow boots. As she limps back toward campus, we can hear her sobs echo across the ice.

"What the *fuck* is wrong with you?" Vera skates menacingly toward Freja, holding the wig under her arm like a dead animal.

"I am so sorry," Freja says, wiping her eyes. "I am just shocked! I did not know that was not her real hair!"

I skate right up to her, close enough that I can see the

fine blond hairs furring her upper lip. Close enough that my breath, dry and sour from all this exercise, makes her lean away from me. "I have to go check on my friend," I whisper, cupping her face with the pads of my fingers, "but trust: I'll be back for you."

35

THERE'S THIS STAIRWELL AT RED OAK, in the academic building, that nobody ever uses. We all walk around the long way to get from our academic classes to the computer lab in order to avoid it. One day, when I first got here, I asked why.

"It's haunted," Swizzie explained with a shrug.

"Two suicides," added Vera. "A month apart. Long before any of us were here."

"It's only two stories, but they jumped headfirst."

"Swan dive."

"*Splat!*"

I had laughed. That's what you do sometimes when you hear about something awful happening to someone who could have been you.

I am not laughing now.

Madison is missing, and I've already checked our room, the admin office, the nurse's office, and the kitchen. She's not in any of those places, and there is nowhere else on campus I have known her to go.

There's only one more place to check.

I cross the snowy quad, my toes numb through my boots. The academic building is quiet, abandoned. I walk toward the fire door that leads to the stairwell. The door opens with a low creak. The floor is concrete. Head-splitting hard. I look up. The banisters winding up to the second floor have all been replaced with high metal bars, like the slats of a baby's crib. They reach all the way up to where they are bolted to the ceiling. You couldn't jump if you tried. And for once, I am grateful to those who took the time to babyproof the whole of planet Red Oak, to save us from ourselves.

Dinner rolls around, and she doesn't show up. Neither does Freja. Maybe, at least, Freja is being punished, or maybe Mary Pat has hidden her away somewhere solitary for her own protection, like they do in prisons. Smart. I don't say much as I absently fork potato pancakes, made from the last dregs of the Thanksgiving leftovers, into my mouth. I'm thinking. As soon as I'm done eating and washing my dishes, I sneak away from constructive relaxation to my room, which is where I finally find her, curled under the covers, facing the wall. Mary Pat must have gotten her wig back to her, because it's here, uncombed, sitting askew on its Styrofoam head. It's dark except for my desk lamp, even though lights-out is still an hour away.

"Hey," I say from a safe distance. No response. She's crying, quietly. Her shoulders are shaking.

"Madison."

"Please don't turn on the light."

"Okay. I'm not. I'm just standing here. Are you all right?"

She sits up, clicks on her reading light, and turns to face me.

I stumble backward. She's still holding the tweezers in her hand. I don't know where she got them; tweezers are banned personal grooming items, and now I know why.

Her eyes are red and bald as an opossum's, and in a sad, small pile on her wrist sits a collection of tiny hairs.

She runs a finger along the pale arched line of skin where one of her eyebrows used to be.

"I only wanted to do a little," she says. "And then I just couldn't stop."

"It's okay." I'm trying not to stare at her gigantic forehead. So *that's* the point of eyebrows, I realize suddenly. It's to make you forget that your eyes, nose, and mouth only take up 50 percent of the acreage of your face. "I get it. You were upset."

"Yeah."

"It's okay."

"Did you know," she says softly, "that I'm the only girl here besides Freja who came to Red Oak without transport? Nobody had to pin me down or force me out of bed in the middle of the night. After the car-bomb thing, my parents just suggested the idea, coming to a place like this, and I jumped at the chance. I thought if I could disappear, their lives would be better."

She reaches up absently to pull at her eyebrows before she realizes they're no longer there.

"Well," I say, "you thought wrong. I'm sure your parents love you."

"No, it's true. My mom is a professor of economics. I'm not what you'd call a 'value add' kind of person. I don't add anything good to anybody's life."

"Listen," I say. "Stop, okay? I've had those same thoughts. Especially after—" I stop.

"After what?"

"Here's how little I think of *my*self." I climb the bunk ladder and sit cross-legged next to her on her bed. "I didn't even know this guy raped me until Vivian pointed it out to me. I just thought it was bad sex. I just thought that's how senior guys treated freshman girls."

Madison blinks at me with round, lashless eyes from behind her outdated pink glasses. She doesn't say anything. All her fingernails are ridged in dried brown blood.

"But now I know, okay? Now I know. I've learned something at this place after all, as it turns out. And, Madison, you count. I mean it. Who gives a shit about this 'value add' stuff? Don't you know that negative numbers have value, too? Algebra stretches in both directions. So does life. Okay?"

"Okay," she sniffs, staring down at her tortured hands.

"Where'd you even get a pair of tweezers, anyway?"

"I wasn't ambushed by transport men, remember? I had time to prepare."

She directs me to a slit she'd fashioned into the bottom of her suitcase, where a small manicure kit, containing a pink nail file, nail clippers coated in silver glitter, and a stainless steel pair of cuticle scissors, is hidden.

"Most people our age use hiding places to stash condoms and weed. Not you, though."

She manages a smile. "Not me."

"Okay." I stick my hand out, palm up. "Fork over the contraband. Your pubic region will thank me in the morning."

Madison sighs but obeys. I slide the tweezers back into the little box and, with a quick glance over my shoulder to make sure she's not watching, carefully remove the scissors and push them up the sleeve of my sweatshirt before nestling the kit back into its hiding place.

36

I WALK CLOSELY BESIDE MADISON to breakfast, feeling more like a bodyguard than a roommate. All the way across the snowy quad, she hangs her head to conceal her new look. Her tweeze job won't escape Mary Pat's notice at group chat, of course, but at least maybe she can get through breakfast before having to face the consequences.

As we line up for oatmeal and eggs, I notice that Freja has wisely decided to start eating her meals with the girls in her own house.

"Damn!" Trinity shrieks as soon as we set down our trays. "What the hell happened to your *face*?"

"Shut up, Trin," Madison mumbles, swirling her spoon muckily around her oatmeal.

"But what did you *do*?"

"What does it look like I did?" She spoons her breakfast into her mouth with one hand, while covering the top part of her face with the other, as if it's unbearably bright in this predawn room.

"You have no *eyebrows*."

"You know, Trinity, maybe if the porn thing doesn't work

out, you could be a detective."

"Is this because of Freja? Because all you need to do is say the word and we will whoop her ass."

"No!" Madison looks up, suddenly, her face frozen in perpetual surprise. "Please. Please don't whoop her ass, Trinity. Okay? I mean it. I'm not even mad at her. It probably *was* funny, me falling and losing my wig and everything. When things are funny, people laugh. They can't help it."

"*I* didn't laugh." Trin looks around the table. "Did *you* laugh, Mia?"

"Nope."

"How 'bout you, Vera?"

"No. No I did not."

"See? None of *us* laughed. And you know why? Because it wasn't funny."

"You know what *would* be funny, though?" Vera says through a mouthful of apple.

"What?"

"If we whooped Freja's ass."

"*Guys*—"

"No, Madison's right, everybody." I shoot Madison a reassuring smile. "There's no point in getting ourselves in trouble and starting, like, a civil war with Conifer House over this."

"I don't know." Vera snaps off the stem of her apple and discards it in her uneaten bowl of Cheerios. "Winter around here is pretty boring. An interhouse civil war might be just the distraction we need. Since we probably aren't going to be ice-skating anymore."

"I hear you, but I think we should respect Madison's wishes on this one."

Trinity starts to object, but when Madison leans down to scoop another spoonful of oatmeal into her mouth, I give her a look. Then she gets it. You don't live in isolation with people for months at a time without being able to interpret each other's most subtle looks. The three of us—Trin, Vera, and me—share a secret smile over our breakfast trays. They understand my unspoken words: *I've got a plan.*

Because of Madison's tweezers, I know that we're in for a room search, the kind Dee relishes, pounding on our bedroom door with one fist as she's turning the knob with the other. So after kitchen cleanup, on our way to group chat, I slip the nail scissors to Vera.

"Hang on to these until tomorrow," I whisper. "Bring them with you to PE."

37

THE LOCKER ROOM SHOWERS in the Red Oak gym are semi-communal; enclosed just enough to pass muster with skeptical prospective parents who come to tour the place but public enough to deny us even a moment of true privacy. There are ten doorless stalls, five on one wall, five on the other, so that even if you can't see the naked girl on either side of you, you can clearly see the girl directly across from you, and the ones on either side of her as well. We are not allowed to use our own personal hygiene products in gym class; a large tower with dispensers of cheap shampoo, conditioner, and soap stands between the two shower aisles, forcing you to step out into public view every time you need to get some product.

The locker room also has five private stalls, equipped with their own private soap dispensers, and we all have the option of using them anytime we want. But nobody ever does. That's because if even one girl requests a private stall, then Coach Leslie has to stand outside the shower door to monitor her—and, by default, to monitor all of us. And since we resent any intrusion on our very limited moments of unchaperoned freedom, Red Oak groupthink has decreed that showering in private is a deviant act. If you request a private shower, you're a princess, a diva, a special fucking snowflake. Or you must have gotten your hands on a self-harming tool—the spring of a mechanical pencil, maybe, or the sharp foil edge of an applesauce cup—and now you're trying to hide the damage you've done. Or you're such a horny little freak that your masturbatory habits can't wait until after lights out when you're sure your roommate is sleeping, like a normal person. Regardless of the imagined reason, nobody ever showers in private.

As a result of this situation, I've grown quite familiar with the bodies of my classmates. I know whether nipples are large or small, pink or brown. I know who has stretch marks and birthmarks and body acne and scars, self-inflicted or otherwise. I know the color and quantity of pubic hair and where each girl is secretly carrying extra weight. I know each roll and muscle, each kiss of thigh and curve of shoulder.

I know Freja's body.

I know the narrow plane of her waist, the round, high ass, the long, smooth back with the single mole directly in the middle, as if, when you pressed it, she might come to life. The breast implants that I didn't know were breast implants until Trinity asked her straight-out and she admitted it. The long, thick hair, so shiny when wet it looks like a cascade of black vinyl.

Today, I've got my eye out for it especially.

"Let she who mocks the bald join the ranks of the hair-less," Vera had pronounced after I whispered my plan to her and Trinity as we crossed the quad after yesterday's morning classes. "I like it."

Coach Leslie is always stationed just outside the locker room entrance when we shower, or at least she's supposed to be, but we know that she's addicted to her fantasy league, and tonight the Vikings are playing the Bears on Thursday night football. Trin takes the shower closest to the entrance, the one that normally goes unused because anyone walking past in the gym can see straight in at you.

She nods at me when Coach Leslie, after hanging around at the doorway for a few requisite minutes, hoofs it back to her office computer to make some trades.

I turn on my shower. I take my time peeling off my sweats and sports bra, where I've been stowing the cuticle scissors that Vera handed off to me at the beginning of class, and which were periodically stabbing me all throughout our bad-minton tournament.

Vera has taken the shower across from me. She is distract-edly rubbing her own mane of scraggly black hair, waiting for a signal. As soon as Freja steps outside her cube for some shampoo, her silicone chest leading the way, I give the nod.

We're on her in an instant, taking her down to the tile.

I feel a flash of pain in my knee as it cracks into the soap tower. It takes me a moment to understand that Freja is thrashing beneath me like a caught fish. Vera, wild-eyed, skids across to her, holding her hands back while Trinity covers her mouth and I lift up the great, sopping wad of her precious hair. I gather as much of it as I can between the blades of the cuticle scissors and squeeze them shut. Muffled by Trin's hand, Freja fights and screams so violently you'd think we were cutting off her actual fingers instead of her hair.

"Shut up," I whisper in her ear. "Maybe next time you decide to rip out someone's heart with your stupid laugh, you'll think twice."

"*Stop!* What are you guys *doing?*"

Madison has stumbled out of the shower, hair dripping, boobs swinging. The problem we are encountering is that we were supposed to act fast, before the other girls could stop us, but these scissors are made for cutting tiny curls of cuticles, and Freja's hair is very long and thick and copious.

"Get back in the shower," Vera shouts while I snip frantically. "Get back!"

"Stop!" Madison shrieks. "What are you guys— *Stop!*"

Naked girls are now creeping out of their various stalls to gawk, to chide, to shout encouragement or vitriol—after all, regardless of how they feel about Freja, this is some good and much-needed entertainment—but all I'm aware of is the fact that this hair is so *thick* and these scissors are so *dull*.

And here is Coach Leslie, looking like a sweat-suit-clad

demon, the steam swirling around her and settling in misty droplets at the top of her white puff of hair, and as I'm being dragged away by her hands and Dee's, who seems to have materialized from nowhere, I feel myself almost instantly drained of the rage I'd been cultivating toward Freja ever since what she did to Madison. Seeing her there, reduced to a sobbing heap on the wet tiles, a small section of hair near her face shorn to ear length, I feel a sick bloom of guilt and shame for what I've done. It's disappointing, really: I thought I was tougher than all that.

38

"GOOD EVENING, MR. AND MRS. DEMPSEY. The purpose of this hearing today is to discuss the physical assault that occurred in the locker room earlier this afternoon."

"Physical assault is a little *extreme*, don't you think?" I interrupt. "We cut some of her hair with *cuticle* scissors."

"As Mia well knows," Mary Pat continues without looking at me, "and as you know, too, Mr. and Mrs. Dempsey, here at Red Oak we have a zero-tolerance policy against physical violence of *any* kind."

"Yes, we know, Mary Pat," Dad says quickly. "We are just so embarrassed about Mia's behavior."

"Embarrassed but not surprised," Alanna says, her fingers brushing her nose as a not-so-subtle reminder of what I'm capable of.

"Does this mean you're kicking me out?" I ask. "Because I can have my bag packed in five minutes."

"Mia, give it a rest!" my dad snaps. "You think this is funny?"

"No, I don't think it's funny. I didn't think it was funny when my roommate pulled out all her eyebrows alone in her bed. Or when she told me she doesn't matter and she hates herself. And I don't see *Freja* having a disciplinary hearing over that."

"Mia," Vivian says, "you don't need to concern yourself with Freja's consequences. We're here to talk about *you*."

"Yeah, well, I'm sick and fucking tired of talking about *me*. I've had about as much self-exploration as I can handle. So let's just cut to the chase. Are you gonna kick me out or not?"

"I'm sure you'd love that," Dad says, "but you're not getting off that easy, kid."

"Cool, well, in that case, I'll just chill here until Vivian decides, based on completely subjective factors, that I'm 'cured.' Or until you guys run out of money. Which won't be very long now."

"As a matter of fact, smart-mouth," says Alanna, "we have *plenty* of money to pay your tuition."

"Bullshit!" I laugh. "I know how much you make. I know how much Dad makes. I know what this place costs per month. And I'm better at math than you are."

"You think you're smarter than everyone, don't you? But you don't know everything. Not by a mile."

"Alanna—"

I watch as Dad puts a hand on her arm and gives her a look.

"What?" she snaps.

Something weird is going on here. Her smug, secretive face. His look of rising panic.

"What's going on?" I demand.

"Tell her!"

"Jesus, Alanna. This is not the time nor the place." Dad rubs his hands over his face and leans back against the couch.

"Uh, Mr. and Mrs. Dempsey," says Mary Pat. "If we could get back to the matter at hand—"

"Time nor the place for what?" I interrupt.

Dad shoots Alanna a withering look, which I would have enjoyed much more if it weren't for this feeling that's now lodged itself in the middle of my stomach, as hard and knotty as a peach pit.

"*What?*"

Dad glances over at Vivian, who nods at him, almost imperceptibly. Which is when I realize that whatever secret it is that he's holding, I'm the only one in this room who isn't already privy to it.

"Mia, we have to tell you something," he says. "And you're not going to like it."

I stare at the screen, at the face that is a digital approximation of his face, the Wi-Fi around here not high enough quality to capture the nuances of his tired familiar eyes.

"This is a valuable discussion to have," Mary Pat bleats, "but right now we've convened to discuss Mia's consequences."

I ignore her. My dad does, too. Allies, still, despite everything.

"We've had some—ah—financial assistance with your Red Oak tuition, honey."

"Okay," I say slowly. "You mean like a scholarship?"

"Not exactly." He runs his hands through his hair again and stares up at the ceiling. "It's— Christ. Okay. We— Your mom had a life insurance policy."

I stare at him. "And?"

"And." He clears his throat. "It was for a lot of money. That's a relative term, honey," he adds quickly. "For some of your new friends, it wouldn't mean much. It's not in the millions or anything. But it's a lot for us. And since it paid out, when you were a little girl, I've just sort of . . . sat on it. I thought that spending it would feel like we were monetizing her. Like we were giving pieces of her away. But then I realized that she is *gone*, Mia. She's never coming back. She bought that policy to take care of you. And here you were, wild, out of control, and I was losing you, and I thought—she would want this. This is how I should spend that money."

"Mom's life insurance." I repeat the words dully.

"When you finish here or—or reach maturation, or whatever they call it—there should still be some left to help pay for your college. And that's what I'm—that's what I'd love to spend the rest on."

I don't know why I'm so upset. He's right—she's gone. She's dead. She's been dead forever. She's been dead so long she might as well never have been alive. But still. It feels so terribly wrong. Like a desecration of the very little I have left of her. I close my eyes and reach for breaths, the way I've been taught to do, which is so much harder and less effective than pills that I don't know why anybody ever bothers.

"So the only reason you have this money," I finally say, "is because mom got murdered. This is her death money."

"It's not—I don't want you to think of it that way."

He looks to Alanna to back him up, but she, for once, is silent. She squirms uncomfortably and stares at her French manicure.

"And you *took* that money?" I turn on Vivian and Mary Pat now. "You knew where it came from, and you *took* it?"

"Mia—" Vivian tries to put a hand on mine, but I yank it away.

"Don't *touch* me. You're *disgusting*. Taking dirty money that only exists because a man put his hands around my mother's neck and squeezed until she was dead? And then threw her in the ocean like a piece of trash? So much for smashing the patriarchy, right? You think that if you don't say anything, that if you keep it a secret, that absolves you? You're like some *mob* wife. As long as the money's flowing, you don't give a shit. That's what you both are. Fucking mob wives."

"I understand you're angry," Vivian says softly, "but I think that's an extremely imperfect analogy."

"Fuck you, Vivian. You don't *understand* anything about me."

"Mia," Dad pleads. "I knew your mom better than you did. She would have wanted this. She wouldn't have wanted you throwing away your potential, your gifts, running around with these . . . these *losers* the way you—"

Because I know they're probably true, his words make my heart dry up.

"You don't need to worry about me, Dad," I say as calmly as I can, pushing away from the table and standing up. "I have better taste in men than Mom did."

I turn away from his face on the screen. I turn my back on him, just like he did to me that October day when he hired those transport meatheads to come take me away.

39

IT'S FREEZING OUTSIDE, and I'm not dressed for it because I was planning on just going to this stupid disciplinary hearing and then back to my dorm, but instead I go for a walk in the woods.

The cattails are frozen, the fronds snapped off by the wind or buried under the snow. The lake is a frozen coin surrounded by a parabola of dark green fir trees. The sky is so heavy with gray clouds it looks like it's ready to sag onto the treetops. And everywhere around me, this true forest silence, as round and shimmering as a bubble.

It's this silence that I just can't stand. I imagine my mother, Allison Dempsey, young, gorgeous, the type of woman who doesn't love being *a* mom but who loves being *my* mom, walking into some financial office and buying insurance for herself, just in case something awful happens to her, because she knows herself, she knows that she is reckless and stupid and wild, and even if she's not willing to change her behavior, she's at least willing to be take responsibility for all the things that will continue happening once she's a ghost. Maybe she knew that Roddie was a psycho; maybe she saw all the writing on the wall, but she still ran away with him anyway. But it's cool, it's fine, it's not her fault: she bought *life* insurance.

All these years, I thought boys were my problem. Boys who push and force and take and laugh. Xander. Scottie Curry. Dillon Keating in the woods. The boys who put their hands on me at the beach or gave me drugs at anonymous parties in leafy suburbs whose streets I don't know. The little scrum of hockey boys who kept making sex noises when I was trying to recite my stupid poem for Poetry Out Loud in Mr. Chu's sophomore English class. *"A savage race,"* I whispered, staring them down with their stupid floppy haircuts, *"that hoard, and sleep, and feed, and know not me."*[24]

But now I realize that when I really think about it, it's the women in my life who have hurt me the deepest, who have done the real damage, who have made me the way I am. My mom, who abandoned me. My stepmom, who treats me like an extra appendage in the body of our family. The girls in school who chased me down, stepped on the heels of my shoes, threw things at me, called me the worst names. Marnie, who dropped my ass when I started gathering my slut rep.

And now I can add Mary Pat and Vivian to that list.

What I've always said—what I've even said, specifically, to Vivian—is that maybe I've given my body away too many

---

[24] From "Ulysses" by Alfred, Lord Tennyson.

times, but the compromise, the thing that keeps me feeling like a human, is that my mind is mine alone. Untouchable.

But Vivian—I let her in. I told her things. I named names, I told specifics.

I cried to her. I asked her to help me, and she did. I trusted her, which was such a stupid amateur mistake. Look how she pushed me and pushed me to talk, to tell things. I wasn't comfortable, and she knew it, but she pushed me anyway.

I should have recognized the language.

You need to trust me, Mia.
You can tell me.
You need to open up. Open your mouth
and speak.

Open your legs
and let me in.
I'm not like those other guys.

Trust me.

LEAVING

I FUCKED UP, I KNOW THAT, BUT JESUS,
CAN'T A GIRL JUST DO THE BEST SHE CAN?

—LANA DEL REY, "MARINERS APARTMENT COMPLEX"

4○

SOMETIMES, WHEN I'M FEELING really low and I
don't know how to dig myself out of it, I tell myself there is
no such thing as sadness or anger. For that matter, there's also
no such thing as happiness or even love. It's all just chemical reactions. The firing of synapses, a shot of dopamine, a
burst of serotonin, brain waves connecting with nerves. Say,
for example, you are betrayed by your father. Or a couple of
senior girls call you a whore on a school field trip. Or your
stepmother skips your eighth grade graduation to go to her
real daughters' ballet recital. Or you find your mom's autopsy
report[25] on some internet site for voyeuristic sickos. Any of
these things might make you think you're sad, hurting, bro-
kenhearted. But I think it helps, in these moments, to remind
yourself that you're really nothing more than a biped, a lump
of matter receiving chemical signals. You can choose to pay
attention to these signals or not, just the same way you can
choose to heed or ignore a walk signal or a stop sign.

Here's what I've been thinking, though: if feelings and

---

[25] Complete with pictures, for added fun!

emotions and thoughts aren't actually real, then what does that leave?

Action. Legs lifting, arms pumping, boots moving across snow.

Which is why I have decided to run away.

41

AFTER LIGHTS-OUT the night of my disciplinary hearing, I wait until Madison is asleep, then sneak down the hall to Vera's room. I toss a Snickers bar, saved from the care package Lauren and Lola sent me at Thanksgiving,[26] onto Soleil's bunk, who takes the bribe and skulks off to the bathroom so Vera and I can talk in private.

"I'm running away," I tell her. "Will you come with me?"

"Hearing went that bad, huh?"

"Worse."

"Mine was relatively painless. But then, my mom's in the Maldives, so she wasn't able to take the call. She passed it off to my dad, who is only too glad to farm out my moral education to others."

"Will you come with me? I need to go. Like, soon."

"You know it's an eight-mile hike through straight-up wilderness to get to the highway, correct?"

---

[26] Other contents: a tiny pair of Barbie ski boots, a used purple Band-Aid Lola got after her flu shot, a smudged self-portrait of Lauren drawn with oil pastels, five red maple leaves collected from the tree in our backyard, and a broken *Frozen 2* Happy Meal toy that still smelled, tantalizingly, of McDonald's.

"Yes."

"And that it's winter?"

"Yes."

"In Minnesota?"

"Yep."

"And that there are bears and wolves and shit in these woods?"

"Are there? Because a forest full of wild predators sure sounds like a convenient story for Mary Pat to tell us to make us all too afraid to run away."

"I'm not saying I'm afraid," she says through a yawn. "And I'm not saying I won't do it. I'm just saying, shouldn't we at least wait until spring?"

"No."

I tell her, then, finally, the story of my mother. What Roddie did to her. How her body had washed ashore at Waltz Key with seaweed in her hair, a plastic grocery bag tangled around her foot, and black bruises around her neck. How her death taught me that if you have no memories of someone, they can't even visit you in your dreams. And then I tell her about my tuition money, how I feel like people are robbing her grave to pay for this shit, and now that I know this, I swear I will die myself before I spend one more day as a Red Oak girl.

The whole time I'm talking, Vera sits and listens quietly, her expression unchanging. And when I'm finished, she looks outside at the dense snow-covered pines, then nods.

"Now that," she says, "is what you call a core issue."

"Is that a yes?"

"Of course it is." She leans in, then, and hugs me for a long time, with arms so skinny it's like being held by an empty dress on a hanger.

"I just hope we can get away with it," I say, my words muffled in her long, greasy hair.

"Mia," she says, pulling back and holding me at arms' length. "In the words of Mary Pat: 'Hope is not a strategy.'"

42

THERE'S NOTHING UNUSUAL about going for a walk in the woods. In fact, solitary nature walks are a practice that Red Oak not only allows but also encourages, due to Mary Pat and Co.'s belief in the Healing Properties of Mother Nature™. Granted, we aren't allowed to go farther than the lake, and we can't go in groups or pairs. But as long as Vera and I stagger our exits, we won't arouse suspicion, even if someone sees us go.

So it's never been a question of leaving, only of escaping.

Our first order of business is to sneak provisions out of the cafeteria—a harder task than you'd think, when you're not allowed to have pockets. But all week, we manage a steady trickle—an apple tucked into a sports bra, a granola bar stuffed down a sock, bags of pretzels shoved up the sleeves of our hoodies. The day before we're set to leave, Vera even manages to stroll out of the lunchroom with half a loaf of bread stuck down her pants—which, given her hygiene habits, I don't plan on eating, no matter how hungry I get.

x x x

We're going to leave after lunch, right before afternoon classes begin. Vera will go first; ten minutes later, I'll follow. She'll wait for me at the far end of the lake, beneath the giant white spruce that marks the end of our walking trails, the farthest into the woods we're allowed to go because that's when the security cameras end and we fall off the map into the great green Minnesota wilderness. This will give us almost five hours before sunset, which should be more than enough time, all things going in our favor, to make it to the highway before dark. From there, we'll hitchhike to Minneapolis and track down some girl named Jenya, Vera's roommate before Soleil, who told Vera, at her maturation ceremony, that she was never returning to her parents' house in Pennsylvania, that she would punish them forever for their betrayal of sending her here by settling in Minneapolis, in Northeast, specifically, with all the hipsters and artists, where she was going to start an all-female punk band named Teen Fun Skipper,[27] and that if Vera ever got the chance, she should come crash.

So we've got Jenya, we think. We also have sturdy snow boots, hats, thermal gloves, balaclavas and long down coats;[28] our store of stolen food, an aristocratic compass that survived

---

[27] In 1964, the Mattel Toy Company introduced a younger sister for its beloved Barbie doll: Skipper Roberts. A few decades later, in 1988, the company gave the doll a makeover and redubbed her Teen Fun Skipper. An updated body mold made this new, improved Skipper taller—almost as tall as her big sister!—with a nipped waist and enlarged breasts and eyes, imbuing her with a sort of sexy ingenue vibe, even though she was only meant to be about thirteen years old.

[28] Red Oak Academy handbook section 4.1: supply list

the sinking of the *Titanic*, and a single tightly rolled sleeping bag belonging to Vera, who isn't allowed access to bedsheets[29] due to her history of suicide attempts. It's made of cheap synthetic material, not designed for actual outdoor camping, but it's big enough that we can share it if something goes horribly wrong and we end up needing to sleep in the woods overnight.

But I try not to think about all that could go wrong. If I do, if I really consider the idea of hiking through eight miles of wilderness in the dead of a northern winter with an emotionally unstable New Yorker and century-old compass as my only guides, I know that I'll lose my nerve.

Vera, meanwhile, seems unperturbed, relaxed, borderline insouciant. When I start to second-guess our plan—the dangers, the conditions, our lack of any wilderness experience, et cetera, she quotes Virgil one day—"'Fortune favors the bold!'"—and Dua Lipa the next—"'Boy, I don't give a fuck!'"

Which makes me feel better. Sure, she's no more of an outdoorswoman than I am, but she *is* a survivor—and one of the smartest people I know. If she's not scared, why should I be?

It's only on the appointed morning of our leaving that a thought occurs to me: maybe Vera didn't agree to run away with me because she's loyal and tough and brave. Maybe it's because she had once wanted, so badly, to die.

---

[29] "I'd never hang myself, anyway," she'd once scoffed during group chat. "It makes you shit yourself. It's undignified. If I ever decide I'm going to try it again, I'm going like Virginia Woolf, straight into the water with pockets full of rocks."

43

LIKE MOST OF THE OTHER GIRLS at Red Oak, Vera and I are accomplished liars. So when the big day arrives, even though my heart thrums with intent, nobody suspects a thing. We go to breakfast, group chat, and morning classes like normal. It's Charlotte from Conifer House's sixteenth birthday, which is a happy coincidence, since everybody is preoccupied with planning the sad little affair being thrown for her after dinner in the cafeteria.

We're right on schedule for an on-time departure, when, after lunch, just as we're slipping out of the lunchroom to grab our stuff, we hit a snag.

"Gals." Mary Pat comes toward us out of nowhere, blocking the doorway with her squat, utilitarian body. "Chef Lainie could really use some help squeezing oranges for the party punch."

"Come on, MP," sighs Vera. "Can't you get Madison or someone else who's actually domestic?"

"Vera, choose empathy. Have you considered what all that citric acid would do to Madison's hands?"

"That's what rubber gloves are for."

"Hm. Well, don't you think if you're going to be *enjoying* the punch later, the right thing to do would be to assist in the labor to *make* the punch? Here at Red Oak—"

"'—we divide our labor as a community,'" Vera finishes. "Yeah, yeah, yeah, I'm familiar with your communist spiel."

We know we can't refuse any further; it would be suspicious and we might get written up for narcissistic behavior.

"Thank you kindly, comrades," she calls as we head for the kitchen, and the joke is so peak Mary Pat that, even though our nerves are jangling, we both collapse into laughter.

Since we're not allowed to handle sharp knives, not even under supervision, Chef Lainie has already done the prep work of slicing a giant pile of oranges in half. She hands us each a plastic juicer, and we get to work impaling and twisting the fruit, dumping the sweet juice into a big sparkly plastic punch bowl. She wipes her knife dry, locks it in the drawer, then pulls over a cafeteria chair to supervise, lowering herself into it with a giant groan.

"Whoa, Lainie," says Vera, pulling an orange wedge free of its rind and popping it into her mouth, "you sound like my grandma. You're not *that* old, are you?"

"Pushing fifty, which you probably think is ancient." She grimaces. "But it's not that. Broke my hip in a car accident when I was a teenager. Got it held together with titanium plating. Doesn't bother me much, but Lord if it don't get sore when a storm's about to kick up."

"A storm?"

Vera and I exchange a glance as I crush another orange against its spike with the heel of my hand.

"Nothing in the forecast. But this ache is more reliable than any weather report. We're gonna get a big snow dump, of that I am certain. *Aggh.* Mia, baby, go get me a bag of tots from the freezer, if you don't mind."

I do as I'm told. Lainie takes the industrial-sized bag of Sysco frozen tater tots from me and rests it across the lap of her checkered chef's pants. Vera and I continue to impale oranges on our juicers, filling up the punch bowl, while Lainie oversees our work with the occasional grunt or moan. When we're finally finished, our fingers stained and pruney, she directs us to cover the bowl in plastic wrap and stick it in the walk-in cooler.

"I suppose I should escort you two to class," she says, rocking herself back and forth, her face a grimace, in preparation to stand up.

"Lainie, is that really necessary? I mean—look at you. You just need to, like, sit."

"You know the rules, kids. Walking around campus in pairs is not encouraged.[30] How can I be sure you'll go straight to class?"

"Because," Vera says, "where else is there to go around here?"

---

[30] Red Oak Academy student handbook section 4.9: on-campus rules—personal conduct: students are discouraged from engaging in private one-on-one conversations with each other during the course of the school day. These conversations, if necessary, should occur within earshot of a Red Oak staff member.

Lainie looks out the window, at the iron-gray sky, the impenetrable trees, the soft hills of untrammeled snow.

"Well, I suppose you're right." She looks slowly back and forth between us, squinting directly into each of our eyes. "I suppose, just this once, I can trust you."

44

"SHE KNOWS, DOESN'T SHE?"

"Totally."

"The way she looked at us. Straight in the eyes. Daring us to lie to her face."

"She must not know us very well. Of *course* we're gonna take that dare. We didn't become Red Oak girls for nothing."

"Do you really think she knows?"

"Soleil must have eavesdropped and ratted us out like the useless junkie she is."

"But then why hasn't Mary Pat said anything?"

"Oh, you know MP. That would be too directly confrontational. Why pass up an opportunity for some organic learning? She'd rather send her subordinate out with this ridiculous story about a 'snowstorm,' set a trap, and see if we make the 'responsible choice.'"

"So you don't think it's going to snow."

"What I *think* is that it's pretty convenient there's been nothing, not a *thing*, in the forecast—which, I'll remind you, we've been following all week. Oh no! Lainie can just *feel it in her bones*." She laughs. "It always amazes me, how little credit they give us. I mean, they've *seen* our IQ scores."

When we reach the academic building, Vera stops and pulls up her collar. "So what do you want to do? I'll abort mission if you're spooked. It's your call."

I turn my face up to the sky, at the dark spread of low clouds and the motionless trees.

"I'm still going," I say. "I understand if you want to bail."

Vera grins, slides her arm through mine, and we break hard to the left, toward Birchwood House, where our packed bags await.

"'Fortune favors the bold,' baby."

45

I KEEP WAITING FOR A SIREN TO GO OFF, or for Mary Pat to come loping after us, her snow pants swishing, screaming about responsible choices, or for an invisible fence to electrify us once we get past the big white spruce that marks the place where the cameras end. But none of that happens. We just walk away from Red Oak: first Vera, then me. I meet her at the tree, and we keep walking. It doesn't take more than ten minutes before our familiar woods thicken into wilderness, and that's when we feel the first snowflakes, so delicate and slow it's like they've materialized in the air around us instead of falling from the sky.

For the first hour, the snow falls gently but steadily, nothing more intrusive than walking through a dust-filled room on a sunny day. The cold is manageable, even invigorating, as Vera and her *Titanic* compass lead the march. We sing songs, exchange dirty jokes, listen to our laughter bouncing off the trees. It feels like we're making good progress, our young, strong, thoroughly detoxed bodies heading east toward the highway.

It's sometime during the second hour that the wind picks up and the snow thickens. We pull down our balaclavas as the gusts toss bits of ice at our faces like fistfuls of gravel. Talking soon becomes impossible, the condensation of breath icing up the fabric of our hats, so I drop back and let Vera take the lead.

We go on like that, silent, heads bowed, moving toward the unseen highway, for what feels like forever. I get very used to the sound of my own breathing and the dark shape of Vera's back in her long down coat and boots, backpack and rolled sleeping bag secured to her shoulders, and everywhere else: whiteness.

It's a little while into what must be our third hour that Vera stops short in front of me.

"Holy shit!" She points up, through the whirling snow, at the high branches of a nearby pine tree.

I follow her finger, and there it is, perched above us on a dark green branch: an owl, white as the snow falling around it, with an underlayer of scalloped black feathers, its beak a yellow hook, its eyes perfectly round, claws curled expertly around its perch. It's staring down at us with a look of such haughty ennui I kind of want to be its best friend.

I haven't thought of Xander in a long time, but I'm thinking of him now as I look up at this magnificent creature that bears almost no resemblance to the stupid cartoon mascot painted on the center of his basement basketball court. What did I ever see in him, the spoiled rich boy with the pocket full of pills, languishing on the bleachers in my gym class? His sleepy eyes, his fumbling touch, handling my body like it was an overcomplicated but necessary vessel in his quest to get himself off. What kept me coming back? What was I trying to prove? Who was I trying to hurt? Did I really hate myself that much? Vivian's words return to me, though I wish I could ignore them: *Some cognitive psychiatrists believe that humans are often unconsciously drawn to the repetition of painful experiences.*

"Whatever you're thinking about right now," Vera says, grabbing my hand and scattering my thoughts, "don't. Just keep moving."

She's right. My life, this moment, is no longer about thought or reflection. None of that shit is real. Only action is real. Before I keep walking into the wind, I turn back to look at the owl one more time, who follows our departure with a steady gaze of disdain.

46

HOUR FOUR. We should be getting close to the highway by now, but civilization feels as far away as it has ever been. I strain to listen for the whoosh of cars, the trumpet of a semi, but I can't catch anything above the relentless wind. The snow seems to be coming from all sides now, and the sunlight, already hidden in a thick cover of cloud, is beginning to dim. Vera is just a couple feet in front of me but I can barely see her. She comes in and out of my vision, the gusts dissolving her like a picture on an old television with a broken antenna. When I try to call to her, my voice is caught and carried away in the scream of the wind. She reaches out so as not to lose me, and we trudge forward, hand in hand, blind.

Soon we are engulfed in darkness. It is not a darkness that city people can even begin to understand. Even at Red Oak, which always felt a little remote and alien to me, there were motion lights in the quad and red-glowing emergency exits at either end of our dorm hallway. Here, there is nothing. It's sort of like the space-simulation booth at the planetarium, but without the fake stars, and without the comforting knowledge that this is all just an exhibit. Here in the wilderness, the huge indifference of the universe has breath and teeth; you can feel it everywhere, but it can't feel you at all.

We lurch on. Vera's grip is the only thing solid, the only thing tethering me to earth, and even now my fingers are becoming too numb to hold on to her. I stumble on something, lose my balance, and plunge forward, my limbs heavy and thick in the snow. I can't feel Vera anywhere. Am I drowning? To be flung through a windshield in a violent car crash, to overdose, to have my body strafed with bullets at school or at a movie or in the school-supply aisle at Walmart; to be strangled to death with a rope, a pair of tights, a stranger's merciless hands—these are all methods of dying that I have contemplated because they are all realistic scenarios in which a modern American girl might lose her life. But I've never considered, up until now, the idea that I could be murdered by weather itself. I didn't know such a thing was still possible, here in the denuded corporate planet of the twenty-first century. I yearn for a Xanax bar, a couple nips of vodka, *something* to take the edge off, but my brain is terrifyingly pure and clear. It understands exactly what is happening to me right now: that we are in the middle of nowhere in a place and a climate that absolutely does not fuck around. The Great White North. The Whiteness of the Whale. *In essence, whiteness is not so much a color as the visible absence of color; is it for these reasons that there is such a dumb blankness, full of meaning, in a wide landscape of snows?*[31]

"Vera." I try to call for her, but my voice is caught in my throat. My breath is coming faster and faster, I can't feel myself at all, and when the sharpness and clearness of my thoughts begin to fuzz around the edges, I realize that maybe it really is happening: I am dying. And I don't want to die; I very badly do not want to die, but it's hard to feel anything right now but relief.

Because I'm not afraid anymore.

I am floating above the membrane of the world. And then the darkness is complete.

---

[31] From "The Whiteness of the Whale," *Moby-Dick*, by Herman Melville.

47

"MIA-."

"Mia."

"*Mia.*"

I open, slowly, my eyes. My head and limbs ache. I am curled in what appears to be the belly of a rotting tree, slick with moss and smelling like the beginning of the world. All around us, the wind howls. Vera crouches beside me.

"What happened?" I murmur.

"You fainted. Are you on Lexapro? It makes some people light-headed, you know. You scared the shit out of me. I almost lost you out here. If you're on Lex, you should have told me ahead of time."

"I'm sorry." I look up, into the intense brown of her eyes, the only part of her face I can see beneath her balaclava. "I'm not on Lexapro. I think I was at some point, but that was like three therapists ago."

"Then what happened? Talk to me. No fucking secrets."

"I think I'm just panicking because we're going to die and it's my fault."

"We're not going to die. At least we're going to try not to." She squats down beside me and begins digging clumsily with her numb fingers through the front pocket of her clear plastic backpack. She pulls something out, opens her gloved hand to reveal a crumpled plastic baggie. At first I think it's drugs. Which won't do anything to save us, obviously, but which, given the circumstances, I also would not turn down. But it's not drugs.

I try to laugh, but my face is too numb to make the necessary expressions. "Where did you . . ."

"Dee led a meditation hour in the chapel last year with some candles and forgot to lock them up afterward. I've been saving them in a rip in my mattress for a just-in-case type of situation. I was thinking along the lines of if I were to somehow happen to come across a cigarette and want to light it, but being stuck in the middle of the wilderness during a massive snowstorm with no shelter but a rotting log works, too."

I swallow the lump in my throat. I thought I was dead, and here comes Vera, with matches.

"I gathered up some dry leaves and sticks and shit while you were passed out. But full disclosure, I don't exactly know what to *do* with them. I'm no Girl Scout. As you well know."

I sit up and close my hand around the box of matches.

"On my honor, I will try, to serve God and my country, to help people at all times, and to live by the Girl Scout law."

"Shut *up*."

"Dropped out when I was eleven." I shrug. "But I think I remember."

"You better."

And I do. The trees are so thick overhead there's no snow on the ground around us, and we form a circle with nearby rocks, clearing a space for our firepit. I layer the area with the dry leaves and some fallen pine needles, then arrange the sticks in a lattice formation, with Vera holding the sleeping bag around me to block the wind. It takes half the book, but eventually the fire catches. When it does, we attack each other with hugs, jumping up and down, screaming with joy. As the flames lick up into the sky, illuminating the bare trees, hissing and crackling and, God, so warm, we lean into it so close our clothes smoke, agreeing that it is, without question, the greatest physical pleasure either one of us has ever felt.

We each eat a granola bar and a couple apples, washing down our meal with handfuls of clean snow. Vera goes over to the edge of our makeshift camp to relieve herself. As she squats down, her pants around her ankles, a cloud of steam plumes around her as her pee hits the snow, and she leans back and howls at the sky. I know she's trying to be funny, but I don't laugh—I feel a jolt zip up my spine, half terror, half love, and I join her howling, because we're alive, and we've got fire, and we're really *doing* this thing, taking back control of our own crazy lives.

The snowstorm has finally passed, and the clouds have

cleared the way to reveal a big, fat moon. We position the sleeping bag as close as we can get it to the campfire without melting the cheap polyester it's made of. We take off our boots and shove them full of dry leaves to soak up the wetness.[32] Then we line them, smoking, up to dry, leaving on our double layers of damp wool socks, and climb in together, curling around each other, zipping ourselves inside.

I'm exhausted to my marrow, and the warmth of the fire and our bodies is making me even drowsier. But I'm afraid to let myself fall asleep. Isn't that when people freeze to death? In their sleep? I'm quite sure I've read that somewhere.

So I suggest Vera keep us awake by telling a story.

"What kind of story do you want to hear?"

"A love story."

"I don't know any of those. But I can tell you about Edgar."

"Who's Edgar?"

"The last guy I dated. The guy who got me sent to Red Oak. One day, when I was fifteen, I bailed on my piano lesson, and instead he picked me up and we drove out to the Berkshires for a picnic with a little tent and some blankets.

"I brought along some containers of things from Citarella that I'd seen my mom serve at her fundraising lunches— Caprese salads, Marcona almonds, figs, that kind of thing. Edgar brought some H. It was the first and only time I've tried heroin. He injected, but I wouldn't. I snorted it. I had

---

[32] Another Girl Scout trick!

standards, Mia." She laughs a little. "It made me feel so good I couldn't stand it, I thought I was going to die. It was unbearable. I get how people spend their whole lives chasing that first high, I get how people would burn down their whole lives, trade in everyone they've ever loved, just for that feeling.

"I was supposed to be home in time to meet with my Latin tutor, but I sort of forgot that time was even a thing that existed. Me and Edgar, we stayed up all night. Saw the sickest mountain sunrise I've ever experienced. The whole sky turned this magnificent blood-pink color as it spread out over the shadows of the peaks . . . it made me cry my eyes out—and you know I'm not a crier. Maybe it was because of the H, but honestly I don't even think so. I was crying, I think, because I knew I had come up against the end of something. And I was relieved.

"We drove back toward New York the next morning, but we ran out of gas in Rhinebeck, and a kindly state trooper who stopped to help us ended up arresting Edgar for statutory rape and kidnapping. My piano teacher *and* my tutor had both called my mom when I was a no-show, which was how she actually noticed I was missing, and she'd called the police."

"Wait," I interrupt. "Statutory rape? But how old was Edgar?"

"Thirty-eight."

"*What?*"

"Oh, relax, Mia. I've always been mature for my age."

"Yeah, but—"

"I mean, okay, would it have been nicer to meet a boy my own age? Sure. But the boys at my school were all horrible to me, and anyway, what would we even do? Go to fucking prom together?"

She's right: I can't imagine Vera, wild, zitty, furiously beautiful and beautifully furious Vera, with some hair-sprayed updo and a satin sweetheart dress, slow-dancing around a crepe-papered gym to Top 40 with some elderly junkie named Edgar.

"The guy before Edgar was forty-three," she says quietly. "I met him on the A train."

"And the guy before him?"

She pauses. "I don't know. He said twenty-four, but I know he was lying."

"Have you *ever* been with someone your own age?"

"Never. I mean it's probably because . . . or at least Vivian thinks . . . it's because my uncle . . . Well, my uncle. He wasn't a good guy."

Her back is turned to me, and my arm is curled around her skinny frame, so I can't see her face. *Some cognitive psychiatrists believe that humans are often unconsciously drawn to the repetition of painful experiences.*

"Vera. God. Did he—?"

"What, irreparably damage me for life? Apparently. Because I'm here, aren't I?"

"I'm so sorry," I whisper.

"Mary Pat talks about the difference between behaviors and core issues. Well, you already knew about my behaviors. But now you know my core issue, too. I would have told you before, but it's so . . ." She trails off.

"It's *so* not your fault."

"It started when I was eight, and it didn't stop until I was eleven and finally found the guts to tell my mom. The last few years, I've had to make a decision: either she genuinely didn't know that whole time, which makes her the dumbest mother in the world, or she did know and just didn't do anything about it, which would make her the *worst* mother in the world. I've chosen dumb. It's easier to forgive her that way." She is perfectly still, her voice even and calm, each muscle tensed beneath her skin. "Anyway. It's one of the reasons Vivian gives for why I'm seventeen years old and have made so many terrible decisions. Why I've never even been kissed by someone my own age. Why everything in my life is tainted."

"Not everything. Not this." I hold her in the sleeping bag, a pocket of warmth in the vast cold wilderness, as the snow sifts down from the branches all around us, making the tiniest whispering sounds as the flakes melt on the fire-warmed sleeping bag. I hold her until her body relaxes, until her hands become hands again and not claws. And then, slowly, she turns to me.

"You're my own age," she whispers.

For once in my life, I know exactly what to do. I put my hands gently on her cheeks, and beneath my palms I can feel the scars and bumps of her pimples, the warmth of her, the long-festering hurt that mirrors my own. As I lean over and kiss her on the lips as gently as I can, I wonder if pain is like an atomic structure. When pain bumps against pain can it create joy? Can it breed love? I hope so. I hope so, so much. Her hair is brittle and sweaty at the same time. Her breath smells like mealy November apples.

"That was nice," she says. "Thank you."

"You're welcome."

Then she begins to cry.

I wish I was a witch, a *real* Wiccan, not an Ariadne/Bron-wynne Wiccan, the real kind; I wish I were a voodoo queen, someone well versed in the dark arts. If I could, I would visit suffering upon Vera's uncle, and then upon Edgar, and the guy before him, and the guy before him, on all the pimps and dealers, the rapists and manipulators, the thieves and traf-fickers and stranglers and stalkers and nasty older relatives who have built-in sonar trackers, pain-seeking missiles that home in so expertly and exactly on the girls who are easy targets. But as it is, I'm just a crazy runaway, a troubled teen, a reformed slut, and I have nothing to give but my flawed, threadbare love, the warmth of my body in the absence of the Rule of Six Inches. So that's what I do: I wrap my arms around Vera and let her cry until her breathing settles and her body relaxes, asleep, into mine. In the morning we will reach the highway, and when we get there, we will thumb our way to Minneapolis, find our way to the apartment in Northeast of some girl named Jenya who I've never met before, and then Vera can be the brave one.

Tonight, it's my job.

48

IN THE NIGHT I STARTLE AWAKE, thinking I hear horses. Galloping, whinnying. But I am mistaken. It's sirens, hundreds of sirens, wailing and wailing like a stampede of hooves. But I am mistaken again. The fire burns in front of us, hot but contained, saving our lives, and out here in the wilderness, there are no horses and no sirens. No city sounds. No animal life but ours. We are astronauts, floating in the blackness. The sky above us is a glitter bomb of stars. I wrap my body more tightly around Vera's and let sleep kidnap me like a transport man, put a black cloth bag over my head and pull me back under.

49

I WAKE UP JUST BEFORE DAWN because I feel something. Something out there in the trees, watching us. My first thought is that it's the ghost of someone—my mom, probably, because who else would bother haunting me?—except that Vera bristles, too.

"Do you feel that?"

It's light enough now that we can just about see the outlines of the trees. Our fire, though low, still burns, emanating a weak circle of warmth.

"Yes."

A streak of something—the movement of muscle. I smell something wet and mammalian—a tang of urine and blood.

"Deer," Vera whispers, nodding her head in that direction. "Maybe even moose or elk."

"It won't bother us, will it?"

"Hey, you're the Girl Scout, not me."

We lay there together, very still, waiting for the deer or moose or elk to emerge from behind the trees, but nothing happens even as the feeling of being watched persists.

"We should probably get moving." I push myself unwillingly from our nest and stretch my aching legs.

"Three miles," Vera says. "Three and a half, maybe. I can practically hear the cars."

We've just rolled up the sleeping bag and thrown snow over the fading embers of our campfire when we see them.

They step out from behind the trees in a line almost militarily straight. Though we are two city girls, we recognize them instantly. They are definitely not dogs, and definitely not coyotes.

They are definitely wolves.

Eight of them, a whole pack, huge and beautiful and light-eyed, soundless, with thick matted pelts of stone-colored fur, their paws crunching in the snow as they circle and surround us. I'm aware, in the spaces between the trees, of a sick blood-pink sunrise. For a tiny moment before the terror liquefies me, I'm struck by the stunning beauty of this tableau.

"Mia." I've never heard Vera's voice like that. It's pure fear. "Mia. Oh shit, Mia. Mia. Oh shit."

The wolves pad closer, their giant paws sifting through the snow. Each one is at least as big as a motorcycle.

"Don't move," I murmur. "And don't look them in the eye."

"Okay."

We keep our eyes downcast, avoiding their impassive tapered faces and instead concentrating on the thick muscular ripple of their haunches as they sniff closer to us. I can feel the biggest one watching me, and I can't help it: I meet its gaze. Its eyes are the same color as the sky, as deep and full of cunning as a human's. I look away quickly, just as I might look away from a boy who catches my eye at a party I shouldn't be at in the first place. The wolf steps closer. I stop breathing, stop moving, stop everything. Prepare myself for what it's going to do to me. Imagine the pain. Imagine the word "evisceration," which I am now realizing is the sort of word that sounds like what it is.[33] The hissing long sound that my skin will make as it unzips itself beneath the wolf's claws, when my chest cavity is ripped open, wet and steaming to the morning, giving itself over to fangs and teeth. *Evissssscerate.*

Meanwhile, beside me, Vera has gone silent with her own thoughts. We stand frozen at the mercy of these eight creatures, our lives placed just out of our own reach, two precious gleaming things on a too-high shelf, like that time with those boys on Lake Shore Drive, like the shattering warehouse skylight. In the past, I've told myself that my body is just a body and that it doesn't belong to me, but now I feel wildly possessive of it. I want, desperately and too late, for it to come to no harm.

An unbearable moment, drawn out forever, and then the energy of the world shifts and the biggest wolf walks past us. The others follow, so close that their paws kick up snow onto

---

[33] I know there's a term for this, but I can't remember what it is. Vivian, the language nerd, would know.

our sleeping bag and I feel a swish of air against my cheek from a departing tail.

Then they're gone.

After what seems like a very long time, we let our breath go. I manage a "holy shit."

"You know what this means, don't you?"

"That we are unbelievably crazy lucky?"

"Lucky?" Vera yanks up her ski mask triumphantly. "This has nothing to *do* with luck, Mia. Wild animals aren't like people—they don't make things harder for themselves on purpose. That's why they only attack the weak."

"So you think they were afraid of us?"

"No, they weren't afraid of us. They *respected* us. Game recognizes game and all that." She laughs, and clouds of steam swirl around her mouth. "They knew we were alphas."

I have no idea if she's right or not. I don't know a thing about wolves. Except that they could have killed us and they didn't. So it *feels* right. Only last night I was so afraid that I would die in a snowstorm, and now, at once, I don't feel afraid of anything. With Vera, I could conquer the whole world. We are alphas. We are survivors. We are not troubled teens at all, but queens of the boreal forest.

The rest of the hike is gravy. Before the sun's even all the way up in the sky, we can already hear the cars.

5 🌰

WE ARE FREEZING, our boots are leaking, we have sixteen dollars and a half loaf of bread between us, but we've made it. We are standing at the side of Highway 169 in the early-morning light with our mittened thumbs sticking out, watching headlights whoosh by through the snow, getting blasted by muddy slush. But I don't even mind. No more prison food or group chat or lights-out at nine, all funded by the corpse of my mom, floating in the shallows of the Florida Keys. I'm free.

I don't think anyone will actually stop for us—what kind of death-wish weirdo would pick up hitchhikers in this day and age?—but Vera assures me that eventually someone will, because we're girls, and as soon as she says that, someone does.

I'm hoping for a woman, someone middle-aged to elderly and harmless, but no such luck.

It's a man, white, maybe in his fifties. A real country dude, wearing one of those canvas jackets that all the hipsters at my old school like to wear, except I'm guessing he didn't buy it ironically. He has a baseball hat pulled low over his face, and I don't like that because I can't see his eyes. The cab of his pickup stinks of cigarettes, but when I ask him for one, he says he doesn't smoke.

"Where you headed?" He's squinting through the salt-streaked windshield at the road as some cheesy Christmas music plays quietly on the radio.

"Minneapolis," Vera tells him. "But we'll go in that direction as far as you can take us."

"I can get you as far as Milaca."

Vera and I glance at each other and nod. Neither one of us has any clue where Milaca is.

We're driving along the highway in nervous silence for not more than five minutes when the guy starts pulling off the highway at an exit. It's a little before 7:00 a.m. the day after a blizzard and there's nothing around but pine trees and snow. Barely any other cars are on the road. He must feel the nervousness in me and Vera because he says as explanation, "Gotta gas up."

"But—" I hate the sound of my voice as it comes out of me, so high and tremulous and weak. I clear my throat. We're alphas, Vera and me: even the wolves knew that. And if the wolves understood that, so will this guy. I try again, louder, firmer. "Your gas tank is full, dude."

He glances down at the dash, and I see the tightening of his gray-stubbled jaw. "Gas gauge is broken. I just have to keep track in my head of when I need gas. And I need gas."

We've pulled off the highway onto a two-lane road, and there is no one around, no one at all. The man is driving fast—over eighty miles an hour, unless his speedometer is broken too, and the salt is spraying up onto his windshield, caking it, and his windshield wipers are flying. For the second time today—and it's barely past sunrise—I'm scared for my life. But this kind of fear is far more familiar than what we faced with the wolves. Hereditary suffering: I wonder what went through my mom's mind the moment she realized Roddie was going to kill her.

Vera, who's sitting between us in the bench cab, reaches over and squeezes my hand. Her fingers are clammy, and her lower lip is trembling. We are lizard brain now, just like we were in the woods. She's in my head. She knows what I'm thinking, and that's a comfort. Unlike my mom, I don't have to do this alone.

But then, the most beautiful sight I've ever seen: a Shell sign in the distance. The man pulls in, and we park up under the neon glow.

"I won't be but a minute," he says, climbing down from the cab, and as soon as he slams the door Vera and I turn to each other.

"Bad vibes?"

"Majorly bad vibes," I agree. And as we say this, just before he disappears inside the station, the guy turns back, clicks something on his keychain, locking us in from the outside. We're trapped in the filthy cab of his truck, and it smells like stale smoke and farts, and oh God, let me be torn apart by wolves rather than die like my mother did, at the hands of a man she thought she could trust.

If someone, anyone, would pull into this godforsaken snowbank and get some gas we could pound on the window, scream for help. But no one comes. What kind of psycho would be out in this cold at this time of day? Anyone normal, anyone who *isn't* a troubled teen runaway or a serial killer in search of his prey, would be curled up warm in bed.

"We need to make a plan," Vera says, reading my mind. "We need to figure out a way to—"

The snap of the door locks, and the squeal of the driver's side door. A roasted smell, rich, heavy with memory—

"Thought you girls looked hungry." He hands up to us first a plastic box filled with doughnut holes and then a drink holder containing three steaming cups of coffee.

"You brought us . . . *coffee*?" Vera's voice is full of wonder.

The doughnuts are greasy as hell, good old-fashioned gas-station fare, covered in a thick layer of powdered sugar. Not to disparage Chef Lainie's egg-white omelets or anything, but, well, sometimes you just need a doughnut. We devour them so quickly I can feel the man looking at us with wry curiosity. But the coffee is even better: scalding hot and wonderfully bitter, both warming and waking. Before Vera's even finished hers, her arms begin to vibrate, and I remember she hasn't had a drop of caffeine, let alone an unregulated meal, in over two years.

"I gotta be honest with you, man," she says now, wiping sugar from her face with the down sleeve of her coat. "We thought, when you pulled off into the gas station, that maybe you were a serial killer. But you're not, right?"

"Nope." The man's eyes are steady on the road now, and we're starting to see signs for Milaca.

"I mean, a serial killer wouldn't buy you coffee and doughnuts, right?"

"I don't know what a serial killer would do," he answers. "Because I'm not one."

"Oh. Well, good."

We drive in silence for a while.

"I mean, don't be mad at us for *thinking* you were a serial killer," she continues. Her voice, normally so gravelly and self-assured, has taken on the staccato catch of an awkward little girl trying to seem older. She sounds jangly, nervous. Maybe it's the coffee. Or maybe it's the fact that she hasn't spoken to a human male stranger since she was fifteen. "Me and my friend Mia here—it's just that we've been through some shit. So we can be a little paranoid."

"Huh."

He leans over and changes the channel on the radio to a local news station. The newscaster is talking about a brain-eating parasite that's threatening the already fragile moose population. A sign at the side of the road indicates that Milaca is five miles up ahead.

"So the big city," our driver says. He sips his coffee. "You girls know where you're going when you get there?"

"Sort of," Vera says. "I have this friend. We're going to stay with her, hopefully. If we can get in touch with her."

"How about Milaca? You girls know anybody out that way?"

"Nope."

"Well, how do you plan on getting from there to Minneapolis? Once I drop you off?"

"We're pretty self-sufficient," I say. "We got this far, didn't we?"

"How far is far? You never said where it was you was coming from."

"Well, you don't seem the type exactly to invite conversation, sir."

"Yeah," agrees Vera. "You're quite the chatterbox."

We both bust out laughing, nervously, and he shakes his head, allowing himself a half grin. We are approaching the exit for Milaca, but instead of turning off, he flicks on his indicator and switches to the left lane, passing a semi in a splash of slushy salt.

"Hey," I say, pointing at the exit. "That's Milaca."

"Yeah, I know."

"But you just missed the exit."

"Wait," says Vera. "So does this mean you *are* a serial killer?"

"Might as well take you two all the way to Minneapolis now. You girls think you're tough. But I've never seen two more lost-looking sheep."

51

WE ROLL INTO MINNEAPOLIS in the full yellow light of a winter morning. Our driver pulls his truck into the fire lane in front of the Hennepin County Library, Northeast Branch; a brown brick building huddled beneath snow piles where we plan on using the free computers to contact Jenya. The doors are just opening for the day.

"Hey," I say, turning to him. "Thank you. You're a good dude."

"The best," agrees Vera.

He nods stoically, not the type of man who goes in for much fuss, though I can see he is pleased. I reach for the passenger side door.

"Girls, hey," he says. "Wait a minute."

Please, man, I think. *Please don't do something gross and ruin this.*

He fishes into his jeans pocket and hands us each a rumpled twenty-dollar bill. I feel a lot of things: mad at myself for assuming the worst, happy that my assumptions were wrong, depressed because I know I wasn't crazy to make those assumptions, guilty about taking his money. Grateful that he offered it, because we need it. We each stuff our bill into our coat pockets.

"Good luck to you, girls."

I squeeze his hand, which feels as huge and dry and calloused as a wolf's paw.

"Ready?" I say, turning to Vera.

"Ready."

We swing open the passenger side door and step out into the icy morning, the sound of honking traffic all around us like the landing of a thousand geese.

52

THE EARLY STRAGGLERS to the Hennepin County Library are people like us, people who look cold and lost and in need of the balming effects of central heating and good Wi-Fi. We shed our layers of winter gear and pull two chairs together in front of an open computer.

"You do it," Vera says, pointing at the keyboard.

"Fine." I wiggle the mouse and the screen comes to life. I click over to Gmail and await her instructions.

"Um," she says.

"What?"

"I can't remember my password."

"That's fine, they can send you a new one. What's your email address?"

"I can't remember."

"Seriously?"

"Shut up! It's been forever. Try Facebook. Do people still use Facebook?"

"I mean, most people still at least *have* it, I think."

"Well, I don't."

"Well, I do."

I log in to my account. After eight weeks away I am inundated with a stream of notifications. Birthdays of people who I don't care about, invitations to events that have long since passed and that I probably never would have attended anyway. Over one hundred of them, and yet, when I do a quick scroll through, I feel that I've missed out on exactly nothing.

Despite having been her roommate for a whole year, Vera doesn't know Jenya's last name. I'm about to make fun of her for this until I realize that in a place as small and insulated as Red Oak, last names are superfluous, and I couldn't for the life of me tell you Madison's last name, or Trinity's, or anybody else's besides Vera. It's okay, though, because even though there are several more Jenyas in the Twin Cities metro area than you'd think, there's only one with a profile pic of a Barbie doll with a shaved head.

"That's her," Vera says. "Has to be."

I message her.

Hi Jenya,
My name is Mia Dempsey and I am currently sitting in the Hennepin County Library with your old roommate, Vera. Yesterday the two of us ran away from Red Oak Academy, and we just got in this morning. We're writing because Vera says

you once told her that if she ever found herself in Minneapolis, she should look you up. Well, here we are now—looking you up. If you could let us crash with you for a few days, just until we figure out our next move, we would be forever grateful. We're just gonna hang out here at the library, maybe go take a nap on the lovely green papasan chairs in the teen reading section, and wait for your reply.
Your friends (we hope),
Mia and Vera

"Now what?" Vera asks.

"Now, we wait. Probably for a while."

"Why?"

"Because most people in the real world aren't up before eight thirty in the morning on a Saturday, anxiously scrolling through Facebook messenger."

"Hey, you know what we should do while we wait?"

"What?"

"*Get more coffee.*"

Four hours after we send our message, after not one but two runs to a nearby coffee shop, after we've perused the entire teen section of the library, after we've performed dramatic readings for each other from a Sylvia Plath collection I discover on the poetry shelves, after we've puttered around on

Google and discovered a news article about Madison's bomb and the injuries her ex-girlfriend sustained on the freeway, after I pull up Xander's Instagram account and Vera declares him to be an unfortunate cross between Joe Jonas and an emaciated raccoon, after the librarian has gently asked us if we need help with anything, then, less gently, asks us to be aware of the volume of our voices and the tenor of our language, we log back into my Facebook account, and there, like a beautiful wrapped gift, sits a brick of text below my own message:

HOLY SHIT YOU GUYS DID THE IMPOSSIBLE YOU ESCAPED RED OAK YOU ARE MY HEROES I NEED TO KNOW EVERYTHING COME TO MY APARTMENT IMMEDIATELY I LIVE IN NORTHEAST HERE IS MY ADDRESS IT'S THE ONE RIGHT ABOVE LA COLONIA RESTAURANT JUST RING THE BUZZER STAY AS LONG AS YOU WANT DO YOU GUYS WANT TO COME TO MY SHOW TONIGHT???

After a quick Google Maps search, we bundle ourselves back up again, toss our empty coffee cups, and push through the glass front doors into the cold white city.

53

IT'S TWO MILES TO JENYA'S APARTMENT, and it's also absolutely freezing, but after our coffee purchases we now have forty-five dollars between us and it needs to last indefinitely, until we can find some other source of income. No matter how biting the wind and how sore our legs, a taxi is out of the question. Even bus fare would be too much. We're hoofing it.

"So. Which kind of Red Oak girl was this Jenya chick?" We're huddled into our coats as we hurry past barbershops and bodegas, our bodies pressed together for extra warmth. "Bad, or just not good?"

"Oh, I mean, I adored her, but she was a *classic* case of not good. Rage issues. Threw shit around in our bedroom. Got all shaky and screamy whenever Mary Pat tried to single her out in group chat. But I always got the sense that her troubledness was just a phase, you know? I figured she'd eventually outgrow it and one day I'd come across her on YouTube, wearing pumps and a wool blazer and giving, like, a TED Talk on corruption in the dental industry or something. I found it all a bit . . . not fake, exactly. Just exaggerated.

You know what I mean?"

"Yeah." I'm thinking of my freshman year friend Marnie, the time she pierced holes all the way up my ears, our weed-fogged afternoons in her bedroom; *he totally wants to bang you!*; and of how, when people started to whisper about how crazy I was, what a slut I was, she couldn't drop me fast enough. "I do."

We reach a street called Central Avenue NE and turn right, following the instructions of our Google search.

"She was one of those girls where the problem wasn't even her at all, it was her parents. They sounded like a couple of super-high-achieving assholes. You know the type, the ones who basically see their kid as a walking college application with gaps in its résumé instead of an actual human being with, like, an inner life. I always figured that once she got away from them, she'd be fine."

"Well, I guess we're about to find out."

The narrow doorway next to La Colonia is jammed with coupon mailings, plastic utensils, crushed cans of energy drinks and beer, cigarette butts. We press the buzzer. The coffee has pulsed through me, been absorbed, and dissipated, and I now feel overwhelmed with exhaustion, like I just got off an airplane that flew all the way around the world. I can feel every muscle in each of my legs, and they all throb with dull pain.

When Jenya comes skipping down the stairs to greet us, it's very clear that if she was due to make the switch from punk-rock riot girl to power-suited businesswoman, the transformation has not yet occurred. She's nineteen but looks much younger, with a small, spare body and huge dark eyes. She wears her black hair in a buzz cut, hewn closely to her perfectly shaped head, and she's got so many piercings on her face that it's almost like she's trying to distract the world from how shockingly beautiful she is. It doesn't work, though, because I still see it very clearly. Her clothes are all black—tight black jeans, black combat boots, and a baggy black T-shirt with white letters across the chest that read: THERE IS A VOID IN MY GUTS WHICH CAN ONLY BE FILLED BY SONGS.[34]

But when she throws open the door and grabs first Vera into a hug, then me, the smile on her face is genuine—and even though I'm only meeting her right now for the very first time, I feel a surge of happiness, too. And of hope. Maybe Vera and Soleil were wrong when they told me that a Red Oak girl rereleased into the world is basically doomed. Maybe if we just figure out how to forge our own path, away from all the shitty people in our past, away, even, from our own parents, we can have a shot at happiness after all. And isn't this exactly what we're doing by running away?

Jenya leads us up the stairs, peppering us the whole time with questions about Mary Pat and Dee and the therapists

[34] Excerpt from "I Have a Strange Relationship With Music," by Jessica Hopper, from the essay collection *The First Collection of Criticism by a Living Female Rock Critic*.

and Coach Leslie's dodgeball league and Chef Lainie's beef stroganoff, barely waiting for one answer before asking about something else. We follow her through a small front room, bright with winter light and crammed with third- and fourth-hand furniture, and into a yellow-painted kitchen in the back of the apartment.

"Sit!" she commands. "Are you guys hungry? Do you want breakfast? You two are my fucking *heroes*!"

She takes two glasses from the sink, rinses them, fills them with water, puts them down on the rickety wooden table and sits across from us before getting up again almost immediately. Her movements are trembling and impatient, like she's a bird who's accidentally flown in through an open window and can't figure out how to get out again.

"Shit," she says, opening the fridge and slamming it shut again. "The eggs are expired."

She marches over to a cabinet above the stove and takes out an unopened bag of dehydrated organic strawberries and another bag, half-empty, of Cheetos. She opens both and places them in the middle of the table. I grab a handful of Cheetos and wolf them down. They're so stale they're as chewy as toffee.

"I can't believe you guys actually *did* it," she says, shaking her head and looking back and forth between us. "We used to joke about running away all the time—but nobody ever had the guts to actually try! I mean, how far is it to the *highway*?"

"Eight miles," Vera says proudly. "Through a snowstorm."

"Did I mention this: you guys are my fucking heroes?"

"Yes," laughs Vera. "But seriously, Jen, you're *my* hero. Every other girl at maturation swears she's never going home again. But they always do. Not you, though. You're *here*, with your own *apartment*, doing your thing. Starting your band!"

She shrugs. "It's not like my parents gave me much of a choice. When I came out as queer to them after my maturation ceremony, they disowned me."

"They *disowned* you?" I stare at her. "You mean, like, they don't speak to you anymore?"

"Oh, this is an old-school disownment, Mia. Not only do they not speak *to* me, they don't even speak *of* me."

"God," Vera says. "I guess in comparison, my mom's not so terrible."

"Or my stepmom," I add.

"What's ironic is that my whole life, they tried so hard to assimilate into their preppy little corner of Philadelphia Main Line society. To become real Americans, you know? But maybe they should have spent less time learning how to downplay their Russian accents and more time realizing that in twenty-first-century upper-middle-class America, homophobia is just fucking gauche."

"I'm so sorry, man. You must hate them."

"Not really." She laughs, though there's a curl of bitterness in her face. "When people ask me what my parents are like,

I tell them: they're immigrants—refugees, basically—who voted for *Trump*. The level of hatred they must feel for themselves is so much worse than anything I could direct at them."

"What time is it?" Vera asks suddenly.

Jenya pulls out her phone. "One thirty."

"Nice." She smiles. "I'm supposed to be cleaning showers right now."

"Mary Pat must be freaking *out*," says Jenya, rubbing her hands together gleefully.

"Madison must be so mad at us," I say. "Trinity, too. Whereas Freja must be completely relieved."

"Who's Freja?"

"Long story."

"I doubt they even know." Vera sips her water. "The staff probably got together and made up some excuse about where we are. They can't have the other inmates knowing that escape is possible. There might be a fucking exodus."

"Do you think they've sent out a search party yet?" Jenya stuffs a handful of Cheetos in her mouth. "Called for backup from all three members of the Onamia police department? Released the bloodhounds on your asses?"

"What I want to know," I say quietly, "is when they're going to call our parents to let them know we're missing."

There's a brief silence. I can't dwell on thoughts of my dad for too long, of him receiving that phone call. It might be enough to make me rethink this whole thing. Vera tries but fails to stifle a huge yawn, a shred of dehydrated strawberry threaded between her front teeth. Now I'm yawning, too.

"Oh, shit." Jenya looks between us. "I'm such a dick. I didn't even think about how *exhausted* you guys must be, after your little caper. Okay, so there are two couches in the Greenhouse—that's what we call our back porch; you'll see. Why don't you two go lie down and rest up—and don't worry about Mary Pat or your parents or anything else. We're going to have a great night tonight. Our show starts at nine. We usually start pregaming around six. We're opening for a band that's pretty big around here—the Lobotomizers. Heard of them?"

We both shake our heads drowsily. I think to myself that I'll have to tell Vivian about this band name, that she'll appreciate it, before I remember that I am never going to see her again, and good riddance.

We follow Jenya out through the kitchen and onto a rickety sunporch built off the back of the apartment. The windows are high and warped and dripping with condensation. Along one wall is an old radiator pumping out huge blasts of hot, steamy air, and two filthy love seats face either side of it. Outside is the snow-covered city, but the glass is so fogged up we can barely see it. A long wooden shelf is crammed with little pots of sweet-smelling herbs: basil, sage, parsley, and cannabis.

"You guys make yourselves comfortable—I'm going to go

get ready for work. Starbucks. Damn the Man and whatever, but they give me health insurance."

We thank her as we both flop across our prospective couches.

"Oh! And just so you know—I have two roommates—they're both still asleep. I'll text them and let them know you're here so they don't think you're, like, squatters."

"Thanks so much," I hear myself murmur. It's so tiny and compact and warm in here that we don't even need blankets. My eyes are so heavy.

"Okay, okay. You guys go to sleep. I go shill caffeine for corporate America. And later we reconvene. And we party." She sticks up a sign of the horns with both hands and leaves us to our naps.

54

BY THE TIME WE WAKE UP several hours later, the sun has shifted and Jenya's roommates have finally emerged, shuffling out of their bedrooms to inspect us before settling down to a shared late-afternoon breakfast of canned chicken noodle soup and the last of the Cheetos. Lucy, the band's drummer, is pink of hair and Scandinavian of face. Esther is the guitarist, who greeted us wearing nothing but a mismatched and not-super-clean bra and underwear set, though she is now clothed, dressed in a vintage baby-doll lace tunic and applying bright pink lipstick in the selfie function of her phone.

The preparty before the show begins just as the setting northern sun begins to flood every space in the tiny apartment with its incandescent yellow light. Two punk boys, friends of the band, open the front door and emerge through this haze, carrying two huge Domino's pizzas and a case of beer. Trailing behind them is a ghostly-looking younger brother who's crashing with them for the weekend. He's got lanky hair parted down the middle like a drummer in a nineties grunge band. His boots are flimsy and dirty, and his flannel jacket, with its matted gray fur collar, is too short on him at the waist and wrists. I sort of feel sorry for him.

The band's bassist is Faduma, a third-generation Minnesotan Somali from Cedar-Riverside, who attends U of M and still lives at home. She arrives at the apartment right behind the boys, wearing a bright yellow down puffer coat and her instrument slung across her back. Jenya does the rounds of introductions, and the little brother is sent to the kitchen to get a paper towel roll, squares of which we all use as both plate and napkin as we attack the steaming pizzas. When we're finished eating, the four members of Teen Fun Skipper gather in a row on the sagging paisley couch to iron out the details of their set list while one of the punk boys, Bobby I think is his name, begins skillfully rolling the fattest joint I've ever seen.

"Hey." Vera, who smells unrecognizably floral after having taken her first private shower in two years, leads me by the elbow into the kitchen. She drops her voice. "Are you planning on partaking of the refreshments?"

"You mean the weed?" I ask. "Or the beer?"

"Both. Either."

I glance down the hallway, where clods of swirling smoke are beginning to drift toward us, smelling like sweetgrass and most of my high school memories. "I was thinking about it," I say. "I haven't decided. Why?"

Vera chews her bottom lip. "Well, I was just thinking that maybe we could, like . . . not."

"Really?"

"What?" She looks at me defensively, her freshly washed wet hair combed back from her face.

"Nothing! I'm just a little—surprised, that's all."

"Well, it's been a long time for me. You were only locked away for two months. I've been at Red Oak over two *years*. That's two years sober. And it's not that I don't *want* to get all kinds of fucked up, but I . . ."

"It's okay," I say, and I'm surprised to find that I mean it. After all, how many of my worst nights began with the snap of a lighter, the hiss of a cap twisting off a bottle? "You don't have to explain. I got you. We're free forever now, right? We can party whenever we want. Doesn't have to be today."

She leans her wet head against my shoulder. "Are you sure you don't mind?"

I push her off me teasingly. "Of course I don't mind. It's not like I'm some addict. And anyway, isn't being straight-edge, like, a rebellion against rebellion?"

"Yeah. Like *not* having tattoos."

"Or *not* sleeping around with losers."

"Or *not* being sent away to a therapeutic boarding school for troubled teens."

"So it's decided. We'll be straight-edge tonight. And tomorrow. And for as long as you want after. Whatever happens, we do it together."

"Cool," Vera says quietly. She slips her arm into my mine, and together we return down the hallway, back into the fug of pizza and drugs.

55

CAN I BE REAL for a second? Teen Fun Skipper is not a great band. They're not even a good band. I've heard better in the basements of high school parties.

But honestly, it doesn't even matter.

They're loud and earnest and they have energy. And I'm dancing in a nightclub with greasy fogged-up windows, creaky ancient wooden floors, and walls layered in the scrawled message of decades of people who partied here before me. It's 9:45 p.m., and if I were still at Red Oak, I'd already be in bed. Vera's arm is around my neck, and even though we don't know the words to Teen Fun Skipper's unpolished songs, nobody in this crowd, who are mostly here to see the Lobotomizers anyway, does, either. It's enough to pick up the choruses and volley them back to the stage as loudly as we can, to feel the screech of guitar feedback in the nerves of our teeth.

I'm having so much fun I almost forget that I'm completely sober.

I'm having so much fun I almost forget to think about my

dad, who must know by now that I'm missing, and must be freaking the fuck out.

I'm having so much fun I almost forget to think about my sisters, who surely are being shielded from this information but must understand, with the precise intuition of their five-year-old minds, that something is terribly wrong.

I'm having so much fun I almost forget to think about Vivian, who must be frantic, and I'm having so much fun I almost forget to think about Freja huddled, sobbing, on the tiles in the middle of the locker room showers, how good it felt to bully her back in her place, and how bad it felt as soon as it was over.

I'm having so much fun I almost forget to think of my mom's insurance money, how Dad used it to speak for her so that it feels like she's been raised from the dead just to punish me all over again.

Almost.

At the end of their set, the girls do a sped-up punk cover of "Sweet Caroline," and it's actually kind of fantastic. I remember that song from Dad and Alanna's wedding.[35] How the whole crowd put their arms around each other in a huge circle on the dance floor, and all the grown-ups knew the words, everyone except me because I was the only kid there, and Alanna laughing under the heavy, protective weight of

---

[35] And probably every other wedding in the history of weddings.

Dad's arm, a protection that I was determined to pretend I didn't mind sharing, and me on the other side of the circle, sandwiched between two of Alanna's work friends, watching them, separate.

"*Sweet Caroline!*" all the grown-ups had shouted. *Bah bah bah.* "*Good times never seemed so good!*" *SO GOOD! SO GOOD! SO GOOD!*

At the time, I had cringed at their hopelessly cheesy adulthood. But right now I'm shouting along with Vera like it's the greatest song anyone's ever written.

So good! So good! So good!

That's when I see him.

He's pushing his way through the crowd and then is again absorbed by it, so I only glimpse him for a moment. Skinnier than I remember, and dressed in a Macalester sweatshirt, flood jeans, and a bowl haircut—college has taught him, I guess, to lean in to his innate nerdiness, sprinkle in some self-awareness and irony, and come out the other side a full-blown hipster. The kind of woke guy who goes to all-girl punk shows. Then again, maybe he's only here because of the girl who was just holding his hand and whose neck he is now nuzzling, with her flesh-colored plastic glasses and hair pulled high to show off her blue-dyed undercut. I wonder if she's the same girlfriend he had when we had our one night of whatever, or if it's someone new.

One night of whatever? I imagine Vivian standing by my

side right now, her notepad in hand, her eyes scanning the crowd between him and me. *Don't call it whatever, Mia. Call it what it was. The winter night that boy raped you, when you were four months into fourteen.*

Scottie Curry. College coed. Living his life. Making his goals. Going on dates. While I'm—what—a homeless runaway deemed unfit for the real world. What made him pick me? Was it just bad luck, getting stuck with him as my lab partner? Or did he choose me? Is it really like Vera says, that trauma trickles down from mother to daughter, stains you like invisible ink, marking you as easy prey for certain cruel and clever boys and men?

I touch Vera's hand.

"I'll be right back," I tell her.

I squeeze through the crowd, circle as close as I dare. I don't want to talk to him. I don't know what I want to do— maybe just be sure that it's really him, here, in the same room as me. I'm about five people away from him when Esther rips out the last three chords of the song—*bah, bah, bah!*—and the crowd goes nuts, and someone pushes me forward so that I trip and knock straight into him and his girlfriend.

He turns around, annoyed, and I brace myself for whatever is coming, except nothing is coming, because it's not him.

It's just a different tall skinny white guy with big ears. He looks nothing like Scottie. It was all in my head, all in my mind, all in one of the broken doorways of my past that refuses to shut no matter how many times I slam it.

"Watch where you're fucking going," snaps the girl, and I become liquid rage, squeeze my fingers into fists, I'm about to destroy her, because I hate myself for still being afraid of him, for still seeing his ghost, hate Vivian for stirring it all up in me and making me face it, *RAPE*, I want to scream in this girl's face, *Do not fuck with me, you don't know what I've been through and the things that I've done.*

"Hey." There's a hand on my shoulder and I jump. My heart is wild in my chest. Not-Scottie and his girlfriend have returned their attention to the stage and forgotten me already. I turn around and it's the paper towel gopher, Bobby's younger brother from Jenya's preparty.

"Hey."

"You okay?"

"Yeah. Fine. Why?"

"You wanna see something insane?"

"Um—"

But he's already tapping away at his phone, then holding the screen up to my face. I'm looking at his Facebook feed, at a post from ABC 5, the local news station. I'm seeing the word "MISSING." I'm seeing two photographs, side by side—Vera looking younger and better groomed, dressed in a white school uniform polo shirt, and me, my most recent yearbook photo, a photo that, incidentally, I despise, because I look like the living embodiment of the smirking emoji and my hair is all frizzy because it rained that day when I was walking to school.

"Shit," I whisper.

"Too bad there's no reward listed," Bobby's brother jokes. "Otherwise I'd have to turn you in."

"Funny," I say flatly. I consider borrowing his phone and texting my dad to tell him I'm okay. That I'm not missing. But if I do that, the police will be able to trace my location. They'll come busting in here and drag us back to Red Oak. I can't do that, after how far we've come. I can't do that to Vera. I hate it, but he's just going to have to suffer for a little bit longer until I can figure out a plan.

I hand the phone back to Bobby's brother.

"Are you sure you're okay?" he asks. "You look a little freaked out."

"Uh, yeah—I mean, I'm, like, a missing person. Police resources are being engaged, right at this minute, to track me down."

"Well, I guess you might as well have fun before they catch you."

He raises the hem of his PUP T-shirt, and I see the metal shape nestled in the space between his jeans and underwear.

"You snuck in a flask? What's in it?"

"Gin." His lip curls into a smile that isn't terribly unattractive. Good teeth, no braces. "It was all I was able to steal from my grandpa."

I want to—the easy escape that comes with it. The way

everything seems to matter less. How fast it works, and how reliable the effects. And if I'd made the promise to anyone else in the world, I would break it right now, without thinking twice. But with Vera, it's different.

I shake my head. "Thanks, but I'm good."

He shrugs, pulls the flask from his waistband and takes a long swig.

"Listen," I say. "I have to go find my friend."

"Sure." He takes another sip. "But good luck finding her in this crowd."

Teen Fun Skipper's set is over, and they've disappeared backstage while the new band sets up. I scan the crowded, hot room looking for Vera, but in my periphery, always in my periphery, I'm looking for Scottie, too. And Xander. And Dillon Keating. I'm looking for all of them, if they could just give me a minute to stand in front of them and say: *I'm more than you ever gave me credit for.* I walk in circles around the edges of the club, my feet sweltering in my snow boots, since as gifted as everybody once said I was, I didn't even think far enough ahead in our escape plan to pack a pair of normal shoes. I thought so much about how to *get* here that I neglected to plan for how to *live* here. But now that I know my picture and name are splashed across the evening news, it's way too late to try to go back.

She's not in the bathroom—I call her name and look

underneath every stall, getting cursed out several times in the process. Finally I give up and squeeze my way to the front, where Jenya and the other girls, flushed and sweaty from their set, have now gathered to watch the Lobotomizers warm up.

"Hey," I yell into Jenya's ear, "have you seen Vera anywhere?"

"Oh, she left." She rubs a delicate hand back and forth across the stubble of her perfectly shaped head, keeping her eyes on the stage.

"What?"

"She left. After our set."

"Sorry. She *left*?"

"Yeah, she said something about being tired." Jenya turns and looks at me. "She didn't look upset or anything. She was smiling. Don't worry about it."

So much for being in this together. I mean, I get it: she's been going to forced bed, like a kindergartener, at nine every night, and it's currently almost eleven. But, fuck, she could have at least told me she was *leaving*. I mean, has she been out of the real world so long she's forgotten the cardinal rule of female friendship: you never abandon each other to face the night alone? Hasn't she considered what could happen to me? What I could do?

I return to the back wall, and Bobby's younger brother is still standing where I left him.

"Hey. Did you drink all the gin already?"

He smiles and lifts his shirt hem again.

I accept the flask, warm from the heat of his pubic bone.

That first sip of hard liquor is always like kissing someone you don't love with your eyes wide open. It's clean and astringent and it slices away your illusions. It's only the next sip, and the one after that, and after that, that start to layer the illusions back in. But that first sip: it's the only honest one you'll ever get.

"What'd you say your name was again?" I manage the words as the burn of the liquor ignites my throat.

"I didn't, but it's Isaiah."

"Oh. Like the prophet."

He raises an eyebrow. "You're religious?"

"No." I laugh. Sip. "I just recognize that name from my mom's funeral program."

"Oh." He blinks and accepts his flask back. "Sorry about your mom."

"It's fine." I lean against the damp, sticky wall. "She was never a part of my life. I don't even remember her."

He seems relieved. I'm very good at making boys feel comfortable. He smiles at me again, for a beat longer than before, and I know, clear and easy, where this night is headed. He taps the flask. "You wanna help me kill this thing?"

56

THE LOBOTOMIZERS COME OUT SWINGING,
lashing into a set full of relentless drums and authoritative gui-
tars. The crowd, worked up by Teen Fun Skipper and frothing
to take it to the next level, pours en masse into the mosh pit. I'm
grabbing Isaiah by the hand, flinging myself headlong into the
pit, and as soon as I'm there, I add Vera to the list of people I'm
almost forgetting about. I throw my body against the bodies
of others, thrash my head until my ears ring. My hair, wet with
sweat and spilled beer, thwacks against my shoulders, flings
droplets. I unzip myself and step out of my own body, throw
it around as if it doesn't belong to me at all. When I fall to
the floor, banging my knee so hard I see stars, when an elbow
checks me in my spine, I remind myself that the mechanics
of physical pain are the same as those of emotion: pain is not
real, it is only brain signals firing, and if you're tough enough
or drunk enough, you can just choose to ignore it.

Someone hands me a foamy half-finished beer; I slug back
as much as I can and hurl the rest toward the stage. Two
palms shove my back and I pitch forward, knocking over
another stranger.

Different hands help me up. "Whoa." Isaiah is grinning, his face ghoulish and chiseled. "You just don't give a fuck, do you?"

I swish my head back and forth as he pulls me toward him by my belt loops. His mouth on my mouth, hot, sour, and strange. It's not like what Vivian told me to see for my future. But that's okay. It doesn't have to be. It can just be what it is: fun, available, now. If he could only be just a little bit better than the others. I would be okay with that, if he could only be just that little bit better. Maybe that's how it works with boys; maybe each one is just a little bit better than the last, until you find the one who makes you forget about all the other beds and bodies that now seem so squalid and ridiculous.

His kisses are deeper now, and the amps shriek with feedback. *A reading from the book of the prophet Isaiah.* These are the only Bible verses I know, but I *know* them. Word for word, backward and forward, because I've kept that funeral program stashed in a shoebox under my bed with a smattering of other stuff that used to mean something to me. I have returned to it again and again over the years, whenever I want to pretend I remember any of what happened, any of her.

I have brushed away your offenses like a cloud; your sins like a mist. Return to me, for I have redeemed you.

His hands creeping beneath the hem of my borrowed T-shirt as he presses his mouth against my ear and whispers the usual lines. *You're so hot. You're so hot. I want you. I want you. Come with me. Come with me.*

Can a mother forget her child? Can she feel no tenderness
for the child within her womb? Even if she should forget,
I will never forget you.

I look around the room, at all these unknown faces, and I don't blame Vera for bailing on me, not really. Sometimes booze makes me cruel, sometimes crazy, but other times it makes me bighearted and expansive with love. This concert, I think, proud of myself for my empathetic nature in the face of so much bullshit, was probably a lot for her. To be deprived of real life for so long, and then to be thrown into it headlong, like this. I have brushed away her offenses like a cloud, her sins like a mist. And when I return to her, reeking of gin and Isaiah's grocery store cologne, she will have no choice but to forgive me, too.

Isaiah's arms are wrapped around my waist from behind. His chin digs into the hollow of my shoulder.

"Let's get out of here," he murmurs.

I don't ask why because I know why, and I don't ask where because self-immolating stupidity is part of the adventure. If you're not willing to wager your whole life for the off-chance of a good time, you've got no right to call yourself a Troubled Teen. And so I jump happily off the cliff, gripping his unfamiliar hand, out of the steamy club and into the snow toward wherever it is that we are going.

57

ISAIAH'S BROTHER'S APARTMENT IS practically right around the corner. A garden unit, the windows are packed to the top with snow. You can't see out. There is a faded gray carpet, the usual furniture tableau found in the apartments of young, itinerant dudes—fake black leather couch, a coffee table ringed with drink stains. A laptop, a guitar, no posters or pictures on the wall. Kitchen counter cluttered with dirty plates, a box of Cheerios, a well-meaning attempt at healthfulness evidenced by a bunch of overripe bananas sitting in a mixing bowl. A duffel bag and balled-up blanket at one end of the couch, on the other, a thin white pillow discolored by sweat stains. Isaiah's bed.

It's not that I don't find him attractive. I do. I think I do? I mean, he's certainly not hideous. But Vivian, with all her prying and digging and questioning . . . she's messed me up. I can't trust my own eyes. Maybe, objectively speaking, he's good-looking, but do I, personally, find him attractive? I don't know. I can't say. And if I can't say, then why am I still sitting here on this fake leather couch in my wet socks, watching him crawl across the couch toward me? The flat little pillow slides to the floor with a soft thud. He takes off his shirt. A sad little amateur tattoo of a fish on his narrow belly. Skin as white as hormone-enhanced milk. Stringy muscles, arms sparsely haired. After so many days of being surrounded exclusively and constantly by women, his tall, straight, boy's body seems to me as sharp as a knife.

I put my hands on the ladder of bone that marches from his chest toward his throat, and gently push him away.

"Can we just talk for a minute?"

He swallows. "Um, yeah. Sure."

"Are you . . ." I can't think of anything. "Are you crashing with your brother, like, long-term?"

"Yeah."

"How come?"

"Well." His Adam's apple jumps. "Things at home aren't great."

I can latch on to this, I think. Talk for a little. Then leave.

"I get it," I say. "Things at my house were the same. My dad and stepmom, they're . . ." I'm trying to think of the right adjective, but before I can locate it, he starts kissing me again. Which, I guess, fair enough, you don't go home with a guy you just met so that the two of you can chat. We both know that. And now his head is bowing down, revealing the greasy center part of his hair, and the skin of my neck is pinched between his lips.

Are you saying the sex with these boys was satisfying?

What do you mean satisfying?

Physically. Emotionally. Did the sex make you feel good?

Yeah. Definitely. Otherwise why would I bother?

His mouth has moved down to my collarbone. Trying to pretend he's smooth, gentle, with the neck kissing. He'll be trying to pull my pants down in three . . . two . . .

There it is.

I push his hand away, just to prolong this lie, that maybe this isn't the same old thing, that maybe, by some miracle, I met somebody *special* at a punk-rock show who shares a name with the ancient scribe who supposedly wrote something that somebody read at my mother's funeral.

The hand slithers back this time, with more determination. I push it away and stand up.

"I have to use your bathroom," I say.

He sits up and blinks. "Uh, yeah. Sure. It's down the hall."

There is a buzzing fan installed in the white-tiled ceiling, its edges etched with mold. Or maybe the buzz is coming from inside of me. I stand before the sink and look at myself in the mirror. Sometimes, when I'm in-love-with-the-world drunk, I think I look prettier than I actually am. But sometimes, I'm too ashamed to even make eye contact with the haunted wreck of a girl looking back at me. According to ABC 5 news, I have made the unfortunate, inevitable transition from Troubled

Teen to Missing Girl. I should be worried, should be running scared, but the truth is, I don't think they will ever find me. Not because they're not searching, but because I'm not here. I'm nowhere. How can they ever find me when, even as I stood in front of them, they never really saw me? I close the toilet lid, which reeks of pee, sit down on it. The gin is starting to curdle inside me, and I bury my head in my hands.

"Hey." I hear Isaiah call from the other room. "Are you okay in there?"

I clear my throat. "Yeah. Just give me a minute, please."

Xander used to ask me: *What do you girls* do *in bathrooms?*

I told him, laughing, *Oh, you know. Cocaine and selfies, mostly.*

What I didn't tell him: that lots of times we just stand there before the sinks, staring at our reflections, trying to see ourselves through your eyes.

Allow yourself to imagine something better, Vivian once said to me. *Something that is deserving of who you are. Something better than what you've had.*

And now, because I'm free of her and don't have to give her the satisfaction of knowing I was listening, I do what she told me to do. I allow myself to imagine something better. Not my whole future, that would be too hard. Just a single moment of it.

I close my eyes and imagine myself away from this place and this moment.

I stay very quiet.

And I see it: a time in my life ahead of this time. I'm a grown-up. A *real* grown-up. Not the pretend kind I tried to be in Scottie Curry's bed.

And I love someone.

And someone loves me.

And we're alone together in a cool, quiet room. Dark.

Our hands, our mouths—

And this someone holds me so tight, so closely and so good that all I can think, again and again, is that one word: "love." I think it and think it, *Love love love love lovelovelove* until the word loses its elastic, becomes meaningless, pulls apart inside of me and my body arches, aching, into the last scattered beats of its echo.

"Hey." I've been locked in the bathroom so long that he's fallen asleep on the couch. "I've gotta go."

"Huh?" He sits up. "Why?"

I have brushed away your offenses like a cloud; your sins
like a mist.

"I just—I don't know."

He half stands. "But—"

The word—"sorry"—almost comes off my tongue, but I bite it off.

"It's nothing you did," I say instead. "It's just me."

"Um, all right." He rubs his eyes. He sounds a little annoyed, but he doesn't press it, at least. He's not the worst guy in the world, I guess. He picks up his T-shirt, lifts it over his head. In the split second where he is blinded by cotton, I reach down to the coffee table and slip his phone, bright and unlocked, into my pocket. If he asks me for my number, he'll probably realize it's missing while I'm still standing here in front of him. But I know he won't ask. Which means he won't notice it's missing until I leave. He'll spend a little time searching the couch cushions, his coat pockets, before it dawns on him that it was me who stole it. I figure I've got about five minutes.

I yank on my snow boots, dripping dirty slush all around his front door, zip up my coat, pull down my hat. I lift a hand in goodbye, in preemptive, secret apology, and as soon as I'm back outside in the air-splitting cold, I break into a run.

58

ONE THING I NEVER KNEW, probably because I'd never thought about it before, is that the city of Minneapolis is bisected straight down the middle by the huge muddy churn of the Mississippi River. I discover this as I'm running through the frozen darkness of Northeast, zigging and zagging down random streets to distance myself from Isaiah, my fingers tapping his phone screen to keep it unlocked. When I think I've come far enough to feel safe, I slow down to a jog through an alley clogged with frozen leaves. When I come out the other side I find I'm standing at the edge of the water before a huge blue rainbow, an electric arch in the darkness. The river burbles in the usual way of rivers, but huge chunks of ice, layered on top of each other along either bank, bump up against one another, and that sound is like a chorus of constantly clearing throats. It's the loneliest sound I think I've ever heard.

A few cars pass back and forth over the bridge, but there's also a narrow walking path across, totally abandoned of people. A sign at the beginning of the walkway reads: Lowry

Avenue Bridge, est. 2012. Which means this bridge is younger than I am.

I walk down the pathway, which smells of seaweed and concrete, fish and car exhaust. The electric arches have painted my whole body blue. Standing above open water, with no buildings or trees to buffet me, the wind is a scream. I curl my gloved hands around the steel railing, take a deep breath, and look down. I let myself imagine what the water would feel like. It would feel like nothing. It would be too cold to feel. If I fell through these bars, I would shatter against it on impact, fulfilling the destiny I escaped that night in the back of a speeding pickup on Lake Shore Drive, that other night on the splintering skylight in Goose Island. I would step, gasping, into the history my mother left me.

Another gust of wind blows up a flight of leaves from the tree banks, and one leaf, dry, perfectly red, lands and sticks against my cheek. It feels like the brush of fabric, of wool, and I remember again my dad and Alanna's wedding. Not the last song of the night, "Sweet Caroline," but the first: "Blue Skies." Willie Nelson. Our song. Because it was me, not Alanna, who he'd danced with first. I remember leaning my head against his suit, his lapel against my cheek. He was my whole world, then. I know now that I probably could have tried a lot harder to be a good daughter. But him, he always did the best he could. And that's why I'm still here, far more a product of his presence than of my mother's absence.

I take Isaiah's phone from my pocket. I tap in to the messages app. My fingers are shaking so hard I have to try again and again before I can type in the number I've known my whole life.

Dad, it's me. I'm safe. I'm okay. I'm sorry, and I love you. More soon. Xo

Then, with a scream I didn't know I had inside of me, I hurl the phone over the bridge.

59

I HAVE TO ASK a cashier at a BP for directions back to Jenya's place, and I'm relieved to learn it's only a few blocks—my fingers feel like icicles and my jaw won't unclench. The streets and sidewalks in this part of Minneapolis are much wider than the ones in Chicago. It feels like I'm walking on a prairie bordered in neon. Nobody's around. Anybody who matters to society is safe inside, and the street is dotted very sporadically with an addict, a huddled shape of homelessness, a yipping and raving man in taped-together boots. And me.

When we first arrived at her apartment, Jenya told us we could find an extra key beneath the stone frog statue on the stoop that is now buried beneath a fluffy white cone of snow. But when I lift up the statue, there's no key. I push against the front door and it squeaks open, unlocked. Vera didn't leave me completely out in the cold, I guess.

I climb up the silent stairs, let myself into the apartment, listen to my breathing, take in the smell of weed and rinsable hair dye and cold pizza. Everybody's still gone. I kick off my boots, shed my snow-wet coat, and pad across the creaking wooden floors back toward the tiny overheated porch where Vera and I have made our nest.

I figure she's probably already asleep, but when I walk into the Greenhouse, I see her fragile shape in the darkness, folded on the floor between our two pullout couches, rocking and rocking.

I run to her, my socks slipping on the dusty floor.

"What happened?" I've skidded to my knees in front of her, gripping both of her bone-hollow arms between my fingers. "What's wrong?"

She shakes her head, gulps a great swallow of air.

"I can't do this," she manages.

"Do what?" I'm shaking her gently. Her face is mottled with tears. "How long have you been sitting here like this?"

"I don't know. I left the show. I'm sorry I bailed, but . . . Mia, I can't do this."

"Do *what*?"

"Be here."

"Where? Jenya's? Because we can always try—"

"No, *here*. In the fucking world. I can't." She pushes her long, tangled hair off her face. "I could have gone home last year, if I wanted. And again six months ago. And again three months ago. But I'm too scared. I just want to live at Red Oak for as long as I can, where nobody can hurt me. I'm a coward. I'm so full of shit . . . I'm not who you think I am at all."

I remember how she came after Freja, pretending not to

believe anybody would ever voluntarily surrender to a life at Red Oak. So I guess she's a hypocrite—the quality I hate most in people. But the weird thing is, I don't care. I just feel this surge of love for her. For putting on a brave face this whole time, for me, when everything inside of her was falling apart.

"You're exactly who I think you are," I whisper. "It's okay."

"I swear I thought I could do it. I thought I could see, just see, if maybe I was ready. And at first I thought I was. But then, the music, and the strangers, and I started to look for you but I couldn't find you . . ." She begins to cry again.

"I'm so sorry. I never should have left your side. I'm so sorry."

"Mia, I need to go back."

"You want to go back to Red Oak?"

Her head sags between her skinny knees. She nods.

"But—are you sure? I mean, I get that this"—I wave my arms vaguely around the apartment, out the windows at the city twinkling with ice and light—"it's going to be an adjustment at first. But if you stuck it out a little longer—we could do anything, Vera. We really could."

"Like what? We have no plans, no money. I know you didn't believe we'd really make it here any more than I did. If you had, we would have thought this through beyond just crashing for a couple days with Jenya."

"I know, but we *did* make it here, didn't we? Not one girl

in the history of Red Oak has ever successfully run away, until *us*. We're alphas. Remember? We can do anything."

"No, we can't."

"Yes we can. We can get jobs. There are grocery stores here, clothing stores. We can wait tables. Or Starbucks! I can protect you, Vera. I swear I can."

"You know you can't." She leans against me as I stroke her hair. "No more than I can protect you. Who understands that better than us?"

I don't say anything because I know she's right.

"Okay." I pull gently away from her and stand up.

"Where are you going?"

"Wait here for me. I'll be right back."

Back at the BP, I ask the woman working behind the counter to google something for me. She writes it down on a losing lottery ticket. Then I ask to borrow her phone. She won't let me unless I hand over my driver's license as collateral. But I don't have a driver's license, so a nice lady in line behind me, buying vape pods and Ho Hos, lets me borrow hers instead.

Two rings.

"Vivian?" I hear my voice, girlish and strange. I lean my head against the cool window of the refrigerated section, staring at the neat rows of milk behind the glass. "It's Mia."

BACK AT JENYA'S, I take off my coat, place my boots by the door, and quietly begin to pack my things.

"What did you do?" Vera watches me, hugging her knees.

"I called Vivian." I fold a sweatshirt in half, fold it again. "She's on her way."

Vera expels a breath, digs in her pocket, and holds out her twenty-dollar bill to me.

"Vera." I laugh. "I don't want your money."

"No, take it. It's the least I can do. I may be a coward, but I'm not a rat."

"You sound like you're auditioning for a mob film."

"Shut up. I'm serious, Mia. If you leave now, you can get on the train or the bus or whatever and go—anywhere. I won't tell them where you are. They can torture me if they want; I'll never say a word."

"Vera, come on." I grab the bill from her hand and flick it away. We both watch as it flutters to the hardwood. "We're in this together, remember? If you're going back, so am I."

"No." She shakes her head. "You don't want this, Mia. You hate it there."

"It's not so bad."

"But you don't *belong* there."

"Don't I? Did you know that, while you were sitting here tonight, minding your own business in perfect sobriety, I drank a bunch of gin and hooked up with Bobby's brother? And then I stole his phone and chucked it into the Mississippi River."

"Well, I'm sure you had your reasons." Vera manages to raise an eyebrow, a small flicker of her old self.

"I did. But still."

She stretches her long legs out in front of her and leans her head on my shoulder.

"So, Bobby's brother, huh?"

"Yep."

"How was it?"

"It was like most things." Our fingers twine together, and the radiator hisses like a living thing. "Could've been a lot better, could've been a lot worse."

An hour later, Dee, Vivian, and Mary Pat are standing in the middle of Jenya's front room, looking around at the Pussy Riot and War on Women posters hanging on the walls, the overflowing ashtrays and greasy pizza boxes crowding the coffee table. Dee's mouth curls with disgust, but Mary Pat and Vivian remain inscrutable as always.

"Girls," Mary Pat says, stepping forward and showing us her upturned hands in some weird sort of peace gesture. "I'm so glad you called us. Is Jenya here?"

"No," Vera answers.

"Hm." Mary Pat smiles tightly. "It would have been so nice to say hello to her."

An adult euphemism for *It would have been so nice to rip her a new one*, I think, but I'm fairly certain my snarky observations would be unwelcome in the current moment.

"You guys are so lucky you turned yourselves in when you did."

"Dee," Mary Pat continues, not looking at her but still smiling tightly at us, "while I appreciate your sentiment, I really prefer we not use the language of the prison industrial complex. The girls here aren't 'turning themselves in.' They've simply decided to come back to us. And for that, we commend them."

I snort at that one—I can't help myself. Plus, it's fun seeing Dee squirm. But Vivian shoots daggers at me, so I shut up.

"You know, it's strange. Of all the nights to run away . . ." Mary Pat uncharacteristically trails off, a look of confusion, maybe even fear, on her face. Come to think of it, they're *all* acting weird, skittish, even. Vivian keeps fidgeting, keeps sweeping her eyes around the cluttered, drab room, and Vivian is not a fidgeter. But I can't figure out if that's just the way they are in an environment they can't control, or whether there's something bigger at play.

They follow us into the Greenhouse to search our packed bags and our coat pockets. As we head out the door and down the narrow stairway, there are no handcuffs to keep us, no hands steering us tightly by the arm. Red Oak does not share the militaristic or patriarchal values of other therapeutic schools—and yet, I have the unmistakable feeling that I am being recaptured, and that even if I tried to run, this time, I would never be successful.

When we're outside, standing in front of Jenya's apartment between piles of plowed snow, Mary Pat guides Vera by the arm toward the Abductionmobile. "Vera," she says, "you ride with Dee and me. Mia, you go with Vivian."

"We can't ride together?"

"No, I'm afraid you can't."

They give us a moment. At least they give us that.

We stand across from one another as a fine snow falls between us like television static.

"I'm sorry," Vera whispers. "Don't hate me." A tear slides down her face and drips onto her scarf.

"Vera. I would never." I reach out to give her one last hug, but Dee's arm comes down between us like a toll gate.

"Rule of Six Inches," she says.

61

"SO." VIVIAN CUTS HER EYES at me as she pulls onto the highway going north. "Was it worth it?"

I shrug.

"You were drinking, I gather?"

"Nah."

"It's coming off your pores. Gin, when metabolized, has a very distinct smell."

"Fine. I'm sorry I disappointed you."

That's the line that most reliably worked on my dad and Alanna. Adults love it when you abase yourself in front of them. But Vivian just laughs.

"Of course you're not sorry."

"Hey, at least I called you," I snap. "We could have easily hopped on a Greyhound and disappeared. Then you'd have a lawsuit on your hands. I don't know Vera's mom, but she seems like the type who'd be big on lawsuits. She might still file one, anyway. I mean, you guys *lost* two students. For nearly two whole days. It was on the *news*."

"Yeah, well, there were other things on the news, too.

Which apparently you missed."

"What, did Madison pull out the last remaining strands of her leg hair or something?"

Vivian slams on the brakes, jerks the wheel, and pulls over to the side of the abandoned road. She whirls on me, then, her face a mask of fury, and tears are in her eyes.

"You know what, Mia? I'm glad you ran away. I'm absolutely thrilled. Because if you hadn't, you'd probably be dead right now!"

"Wait," I say. "What?"

"Forgive me." She presses her forehead against the steering wheel and takes a series of rapid breaths. I recognize the rhythm. She's trying to control her anxiety.

"Holy shit, Vivian. Are you have a panic attack? Because I—"

"Just give me a minute. Please."

I give her a minute because I respect her but also because what else can I do? Teen Fun Skipper, Isaiah's brother's couch, the wolves, the bridge . . . it all seems like forever ago. Now I'm just a Red Oak girl again, speaking with my therapist, confused and angry and most of all, scared.

"Okay." She lifts her head from the wheel, fishes out a tissue from her coat pocket and blows her nose. "Okay."

An oil rig barrels past us, spraying slush onto the windshield and leaving Vivian's pickup rocking gently in its wake. She takes a deep breath.

"We had an incident the night you left."

"Um. An incident? I don't—"

"Your room—Madison wasn't in it, thank goodness. We'd asked her to sleep under observation in the nurse's office because of—well, you know I can't discuss the issues of the other girls. All you need to know is she wasn't in your room. And you weren't, either, though Freja didn't know that, of course."

"Wait, Freja? I don't—what does Freja have to do with anything?"

"Mia." She looks at me, genuinely surprised. "Are you telling me you really didn't know?"

62

NO, I REALLY DIDN'T KNOW.

Some secrets at Red Oak manage to remain secrets. But now the secret's out and so is Freja, ferried away, after a consultation with Nicoline Pedersen and her team, the Red Oak team, and the Mille Lacs County sheriff's department, to a more secure place that's better equipped to handle her particular set of issues.[36]

"But I don't understand," I say dully. "I thought she was here because her mom thought this was a regular boarding school."

"No."

Vivian tells me then, as we sit side by side on an abandoned county highway in the middle of the night, how when she was twelve, Freja was found responsible for a series of small bonfires lit in the stairwell of her elite private school in Copenhagen before she got caught in the act and expelled. How she'd then been shipped off to an even more elite boarding school in London, where she'd been kicked out again,

---

[36] This is adultspeak for "she's been institutionalized."

for the same reasons. Her family had managed to keep their daughter's dangerous proclivities out of the tabloids, had sent her away to be homeschooled by a private tutor at Nicoline Pedersen's remote ecofarm, far off on a dot of island in the middle of the Baltic Sea. And this had worked out well, until Freja managed to set fire to a stable at the edge of the property, incinerating nearly a dozen of Nicoline's beloved Jutland horses.

That's when she was sent to Red Oak. She had no relatives, as it turned out, in Minneapolis.

"But what," I ask, my voice small in the pickup cab, "does this all have to do with me?"

She'd started early yesterday morning, Vivian explains, before the snowstorm began, before Vera and I had started our adventure. During the passing periods between classes, she would return again and again to a little spot protected from snow by the overhanging roof beneath my bedroom window, feathering her nest in the dry winter grass. She began to stoke it right after lunch when the pyre was built and the sun was high. Angled Madison's glasses, the ones Madison had gifted her and none of us knew why she'd kept, tilting them back and forth, gathering the concentrated power of the sun until the dry grass, the pile of twigs and scraps of paper began to smoke—

What a bolt of triumph she must have felt in that moment, as the smoke turned to flame, and she encircled it, contained it, in a little bonfire, small enough to give off barely a wisp of flame, sheltered it from the wind like a newborn, until she snuck out there just after dinner, and again just before lights-out, to build it up higher so as to quickly and methodically kill me. She had wanted to turn me to ash, as revenge for what we did to her in the showers, probably, but maybe not. Maybe it was just another way to feed her compulsion, no different from purging or hair pulling or nail biting or hitting or cutting, this ache, this urge, to turn solid things and people into smoke. For Freja, as it turned out, was the final box on the troubled girl checklist: Freja was a fire starter.

Her fire had eventually leaped up the timber walls of our cabin, come licking in through the window and belching smoke, swallowing and shriveling everything in its path. The fire alarms had gone off first, saving the other Birch-wood girls, and then the sprinkler system, saving the dorm building itself from total destruction. But had I been there, sleeping in my bed like I was supposed to be, it might not have been enough to save me. I might have dreamed that I was a little girl again, feeling my favorite thing, that inside-outside feeling, water misting down onto my face, reminding me how big the world was and how safe I was inside my bed. Our aluminum bunk frame was melted into a shimmering lump; Vivian shows me a picture of this on her phone, as if to prove to me she isn't making all this up. The out-of-date mattress was made of ultraflammable synthetic. Had I been sleeping in my bed, the last thing I ever would have realized was that I'd been wrong about my belief that there are some places in a person's world that really are safe. In this way, I would have died cured of my last remaining illusion.

When she's finished speaking, Vivian unbuckles her seat belt. She reaches across the truck cab and holds me for a long time. I've never known what a mother's love feels like, and I never will—except to understand that this, right here, isn't far off. I bury my face in her long black hair, and now I smell it: the faint but unmistakable tang of ash.

63

WE PULL OFF AT AN EXIT somewhere in the state
forest, onto another county highway filled with nothingness
and trees and snow. It occurs to me that I don't know what
the road coming down to Red Oak looks like. I was asleep
the first time I arrived, and when I left, it was through the
back door. But even I know that it definitely doesn't look like
this: a prairie-sized parking lot bathed in flood lighting, illuminating the swirls of snow still falling intermittently from
the sky. Ahead is a huge sandstone building, glitzy in that
cheap way that makes you lonely just from looking: Lakeside
Casino.

"Um," I say to Vivian. "What, are we playing a couple
hands of poker before we head back?"

"No."

I understand her well enough by now to know that there's
no point in wasting my breath asking her more questions
if she doesn't feel like answering them. Whatever is about
to happen, I'll find out soon enough. I climb out of the cab
and follow her across the parking lot toward the huge set of

revolving doors that mark the entrance of the casino, our boots crunching on rock salt.

The foyer is cavernous and run-down, reeking of cigarettes and filled with the constant ambient ringing of slot machines. Vivian leads the way, walking slightly ahead of me, past the front desk, then veers left, to the buffet. It's a large room, draped in red and silver and gold holiday lights, with a mechanical Santa Claus hoisting his sack of toys to his shoulder again and again and again. Elton John is playing faintly from a speaker in the ceiling—*"I hope you don't mind, I hope you don't mind . . ."*—and it smells like boiled ham. There isn't a soul in the place except for one person sitting alone in front of an untouched plate of roast beef and instant mashed potatoes, hands folded, waiting.

"Dad."

Vivian slips away to get herself a cup of coffee and give us our privacy. I'm standing before him in my backpack and my heavy down coat, my boots dripping around me on this patterned carpet. He half stands, and my name bursts out of him in a sob. He's holding something, some sort of fabric that's black and torn and looks like it's about to shred apart in his hands. When I step closer I see what it is—the burned remains of the duffel bag Alanna sent ahead of me when they ordered the transport men to take me away.

"I got your text," he begins. "Thank you. Thank you, baby. Because before I heard from you, I thought—" his voice breaks and he doesn't say any more.

"Dad, please—I'm so sorry."

I go to him, and he puts his arms around me, and I can't even remember the last time I let him hug me but I know it's been more than a year. More than two. Two whole years. I collapse against him, saying into his chest, *"I'm sorry I'm sorry I'm sorry,"* and I hear him, above me, saying it back— *"I'm sorry too I'm sorry too I'm"*—until we say that stupid word so many times between ourselves it's like we're both breathing into the same balloon, blowing it up until it floats away, carrying inside of it all the other things we should have said but never could.

He gives me a round token that's good for anything I want at the buffet. I fill my tray with lukewarm french fries, a shriveled-looking piece of sausage pizza, and a large glass of orange Fanta.

Dad watches me eat. He doesn't say anything. I realize that I am starving. I eat everything on my plate, then go back for more fries, along with a salad that I fix for myself with an extremely high ranch-dressing-to-lettuce ratio. He watches me eat that, too. When I finally finish, he slurps down the last of his coffee and stands up.

"You ready?" he asks.

I assume he's asking if I'm ready to get back into Vivian's pickup, if I'm ready to say goodbye to him and return to Red

Oak to complete the emotional work my mom's insurance money has required of me.

"Yeah," I say. "I guess so."

"Good." He takes my hand in his. "I'm taking you the hell home."

BECOMING

THESE ARE THE ONES WHO ESCAPE
AFTER THE LAST HURT IS TURNED INWARD;
THEY ARE THE MOST DANGEROUS ONES.

THESE ARE THE ONES WHO LOVED YOU.
THEY ARE THE HORSES WHO HAVE HELD YOU
SO CLOSE THAT YOU HAVE BECOME
A PART OF THEM,

        AN ICE HORSE

GALLOPING

      INTO FIRE.

—JOY HARJO, "SHE HAD SOME HORSES"

64

IN ORDER TO MAKE IT to Saint Ann's School in time for 7:45 first bell, I have to catch the 6:30 a.m. train, which means I need to wake up at 5:45 a.m.—yes, you read that correctly—5:45 a.m. Do you know what 5:45 a.m. in a Chicago January looks like? I'll tell you: it looks exactly the same as midnight. To get out of my warm bed at this hour, with frost lacing up my bedroom windows, the sky pitch-black and the hardwood floor like ice because Dad is currently winning his war with Alanna over the temperature of the thermostat—it goes against human nature. But I guess if you're going to reinvent yourself, this is the price you have to pay.

At least this was the advice of the family therapist Vivian recommended to us after my dad took me out of Red Oak and brought me home for good. We all went—even the twins, who mostly picked their noses and stared with skeptical confusion at the reprint of René Magritte's *The Son of Man*[37] hanging on the wall of Dr. Stuben's office. It was awkward

---

[37] You know the one. The dude in the suit and bowler hat with the big green apple inexplicably hovering in front of his face.

and painful—I could think of many better ways I'd prefer to spend my Saturday afternoons—and we talked about a lot of stuff, which I don't feel like rehashing here. To be honest, though, it was a lot harder for Dad and Alanna than it was for me. I'm used to being forced to look inward. Alanna, for one, is not. It took some work to get her to come down off her high horse. But as much as it pains me to pay her a compliment, she put in the work. She came down. There was crying, there were hugs all around. Feelings were owned. Emotions were named. Behaviors were explored. Personal accountability was taken. If Mary Pat were there to witness it, she would have died of happiness.

It was Dr. Stuben who suggested a fresh start—a happy medium between my old school, where my reputation might as well be hanging in the gym alongside the state champion basketball banners, and Red Oak, where, you know, Freja tried to torch my ass. A place far enough away where I can feel like a stranger, but close enough that I can still live at home. A school that my parents[38] can afford without tapping into my murdered-mom fund.

Saint Ann's School for Girls, which is an hour away by train and has a very large scholarship endowment, meets all of that criteria.

And today, the first of the new semester, is my very first day.

The stars are still out when my alarm goes off, but I'm so

---

[38] See what I did there? I called them my parents. Feelings: OWNED.

nervous I get right out of bed without even pressing snooze. I slide my feet into the fuzzy purple slippers Lauren and Lola got me as a welcome home gift and pad down the hall to the bathroom, closing and locking the door behind me.

I've been back home for five weeks now, and yet it still feels like a luxury, getting to be alone in a bathroom with a full-length mirror and a door that locks. There were no mirrors at Red Oak. A mirror could be smashed, and broken glass could be used as weapon on oneself or others. All we had were these dented metal squares over the dorm sinks, the ones that distort and reflect so dully you can never get a clear look at your own face. I got used to it, and grew to sort of prefer it over the constant scrutiny I'd once placed under my own body. Maybe that's why, in the five weeks since I've been back, I still haven't taken a good look at myself. And so now, when I stand before the mirror and begin carefully removing my clothing, piece by piece, I feel almost afraid. But I know I have to do it. I kick off my slippers, fold my T-shirt and pajama pants and underwear in a neat pyramided pile, and place them on top of the closed toilet lid. I loosen my hair from its ponytail, turn on the shower, and then turn slowly to face myself. It's a bit like a reunion with an old best friend, the kind of friend who has both wronged you and sacrificed for you and who, because of that complicated history, you both love and hate.

Me. Here I am.

My body is a female body. The body of a woman. The curve of it. The cup of my collarbone, the flutter of muscle if I turn this way or that. I've waxed a couple times before—Xander liked it—but everything has grown back now. I've gained weight. My stomach is flat but lacking definition. My waist tapers in, then out again. My thighs, covered with downy blond hair, touch. That's a bad thing, I've been told. But then I've been told that some guys like thick. *Are you an ass guy or a tits guy? Do you like dark-skinned girls or light-skinned girls? Tall or short? I hate chicks with short hair. Too black. Too brown. Too pasty white. Too thin-lipped. Too thick-lipped. Too hairy—that's so nasty, girls who don't shave down there. Moles. Cankles. Cellulite. Small-ass titties. Huge tits, but only because she's fat. On a scale of one to ten . . .*

How do you know if you're pretty?

Is it you who gets to decide?

The freshman girl who walked into Scottie Curry's bedroom two years ago with her tight jeans and sparkly body lotion didn't think so.

But what about now?

I turn left and right. The heat of the shower is steaming up the room.

Many have touched my body, many more have looked at my body, have leered at it, have judged it and compartmentalized it and ranked it on their various scales of attractiveness and acceptability. But has anyone ever beheld my body? Have

I ever beheld my own body? I think of Vivian, her talk of semantic satiation. I say *body* in my head so many times that it doesn't mean anything anymore, just two syllables, two puffs of air coming from my mouth. I say *girl*. I say *woman*. I run my fingers across the fading heart tattoo that Marnie etched, long ago, onto the petal-soft skin at the top of my breast. The closed-up holes running up my ears. Am I pretty? I still don't know if I could say.

But I know that I look good. I look healthy. I look like I've been through some shit. I look like somebody with a future before me that is emptied of everything but possibility.

I close my eyes. I brush my fingers down the silhouette of myself. Before I get into the scalding hot shower to luxuriate in its pounding water pressure and Alanna's rose-scented shampoo, I wrap my arms around myself, just to see what it would feel like to hold the body that is me.

65

Dear Vera,

You better be behaving yourself enough to have mail privileges, because I really hate the idea of my magnificent words sitting all alone in your mailbox for weeks at a time just because you couldn't be bothered to scrub a toilet or do your math homework.

So, want to hear something crazy? I tried out for the soccer team. And I MADE it. I know, I know. I can hear your laughter all the way from Onamia: Mia Dempsey, Student-Athlete. But it's really not a huge deal. My new school is tiny and its sports teams are generally terrible and I haven't actually gotten any playing time yet, but nonetheless, I am on the roster. I have a uniform and my own shin guards. I have teammates who gift me hand-sewn scrunchies in our school colors and who invite me to carb-loading dinners on the nights before big games. And I never thought I would say this, but the whole thing has been sort of . . . cool. Being a part of something, you know? Don't worry, I'm not saying I'm going to turn into some fucking jock now. I'm just saying that some of the things I once thought were stupid, I now think are sort of brave. And some of the things I once thought were brave, I now think are sort of stupid.

I move very carefully through this new life, not taking any chances. I go to school, and then practice, and then home. And yeah, it's boring a lot of the time, and yeah, sometimes I feel the old wildness coiling up inside of me, but I'm trying my best not to let it win. And so far (and with the understanding that everything could have already gone to shit by the time you read this letter), it's working.

Remember that guy Xander I used to hook up with, the one with the rich German dad? Well, he once taught me this word. "Terroir." It's when something tastes like the place it's from. A wine from the Loire Valley of France, for example, tastes flinty, like smoke, because of the soil in that particular place on the earth. It's like how, when someone starts talking and you know where they're from by their accent, terroir is like food or drink with an accent that alerts you to its origins.

You have a very complicated terroir. I would need to taste it many times to find all the notes. The first and only time you ever kissed me, in the woods with wolves sleeping in the darkness just beyond where we could see, I tasted rain hissing against hot sidewalks. I tasted wood polish, clean carpets, and steel skylines. I tasted almonds and money, sugared dates and nail polish, the bubbling kiss of sparkling water, and the chalky numbing pop of cocaine. I tasted the candle wax and sweat of a crowded party in a run-down apartment in the East Village. I tasted something sweet just out of reach, and the insistent note beneath it all, a salt and mineral tang—the taste of buried pain.

I bet you tasted it in me, too.

I guess every one of us troubled girls has her own landscape, her own growing conditions. Some of us came up in the rainy season and had our best flavors washed away by our careless caretakers; others shriveled, unprotected, under relentless heat. Still others were fussed over too much, resulting in overcultivation. And then there were the ones who were ignored completely, left to grow small and bitter and wild.

It's so easy for the world to stomp on girls like us, to burst open our thin, sun-warmed skin. I get why you're afraid to step back out here. But please promise me, one day, that you'll try. And when you do, come find me. There's so much we need to talk about. There's so much I still need to say. Even now, I don't know whether I belonged at Red Oak or not, whether I was, to use your criteria, truly bad or just not good. All I know is that if it weren't for Vivian and you—and you most of all—I'd be a Missing Girl forever.

I see a life up ahead for us, Vera. A proper life, with all the sorrows and the joys, all the bullshit and all the transcendence. I see that no matter the weather or the climate, the erosive properties of the place in which we came up, we troubled girls have to keep at it, twisting and pushing our way out of the earth, our vines green and reaching. If we can just keep going, we can survive. We can prove them wrong, all of them: all of those experts who said we were undrinkable.

    Love,
    Mia

MIA'S RED OAK
POETRY LIST

"The Applicant"—Sylvia Plath

"Crossing Half of China to Sleep With You"—Yu Xiuhua

"Diving into the Wreck"—Adrienne Rich

"Fever 103"—Sylvia Plath

"Get Up 10"—Cardi B

"I'm Going Back to Minnesota Where Sadness Makes Sense"
    —Danez Smith

"In Memory of my Mother"—Patrick Kavanagh

"Mariner's Apartment Complex"—Lana Del Rey

"my bitch!"—Danez Smith

"My Therapist Wants to Know about My Relationship to Work"
    —Tiana Clark

"Obligations 2"—Layli Long Soldier

"Relay"—Fiona Apple

"Praying" (opening monologue)—Kesha

"So I Send This Three-Word Burst, Poor Ink, Repeating"
    —Steve Davenport

"She Had Some Horses"—Joy Harjo

"Water"—Anne Sexton

"Where are the dolls who loved me so . . ."—Elizabeth Bishop

"The Whiteness of the Whale," Moby-Dick—Herman Melville

Acknowledgments

A massive thank-you to the young women who shared their stories with me over the course of researching and writing this book. There are too many to name (and I know some prefer to remain nameless), but I do want to extend a special thank-you to Morgan Feinstein, and also to the faculty and students at Oklahoma Teen Challenge.

Several other incredible women helped this book make the journey from messy manuscript to published artifact. Thank you to my fantastic agent, Sara Crowe, and everyone at Pippin Properties. Special gratitude to Alexandra Cooper, who has now edited three of my four novels and who always pushes me to think harder and go deeper. Thank you to the kind and wise Rosemary Brosnan, Allison Weintraub, Alexandra Rakaczki, and the rest of the wonderful team at Quill Tree Books. This book is a beautiful physical object, and for that I must thank Dana Ledl for her wonderful cover art, Cat San Juan for her book design, and Erin Fitzsimmons for her art direction.

Thank you to Will McGrath and Ellen Block for

welcoming me into your Minneapolis home while I was in town for research, and to Neelu Molloy for sharing further expertise on your hometown. I hope to share a hotdish with you all soon. Thank you Luis Calzada Zubiria and Marty McGivern for your careful, thoughtful readings of an early draft. Thank you Kelly Dunn Rynes for giving me a crash course (see what I did there?) on the physics of ice-skating. Bridget Quinlan, thank you for arguing with me, as only you could, about the true definition of "basic."

I wrote the first scene of this book ten years ago, in Don DeGrazia's Advanced Fiction class at Columbia College. My friends and mentors in the Chicago literary community, many of whom I met on that legendary corner of Michigan and Balbo, have been essential to my growth as a writer. Thanks to all of you, with shout-outs to Randy Albers, Patricia Ann McNair, Eric May, Christine Maul Rice, Alexis Pride, Chris Terry, Matt Martin, Joe Meno, Jarrett Dapier, David Schaafsma, Ann Hemenway, and the staff at Women & Children First and the Book Cellar for always supporting the work of local authors.

My husband, Denis; my three daughters; my family; my close circle of friends—phew. Diving into the wreck of my imagination would be impossible without the knowledge that you were standing at the ready to pull me back up. I love you all!

And finally, a thought about Amy Winehouse, whose

brilliant lyrics provided the title of this novel: however unfair it was, Amy was as famous for her troubles as she was for her musical genius. But it's worth remembering that she was sober when she wrote most of the songs on *Back to Black*. The cliché of the tortured artist is a dangerous one, because pain can't be repurposed into art until the artist is well enough to put some distance between herself and the thing that tortures her. There is nothing noble or romantic about suffering in silence or dying young. If you're hurting, tell someone. No one should ever have to battle blind. And nothing ever has to be a fate resigned.